AN AMISH COUNTRY TREASURE 4

RUTH PRICE

This is Book 4 of the Amish Country Treasure series. If you enjoy this book, please look over the other Christian books from Global Grafx Press, and other great books from Ruth Price.

Published by Global Grafx Press, LLC. © 2015

The Pennsylvania Dutch used in this manuscript is taken from the Revised Pennsylvania German Dictionary: English to Pennsylvania Dutch (1991) by C. Richard Beam, Brookshire Publications, Inc. Lancaster, PA 17603

The Bible quotations used in this manuscript are either taken from the King James Bible or the English Standard Bible.

Copyright © 2015 by Ruth Price

All Rights Reserved. No part of this publication may be reproduced in any form or by any electronic or mechanical means, including scanning, photocopying, or otherwise without prior written permission of the copyright holder, except by a reviewer who may quote brief passages in a review.

Copyright © 2015 Ruth Price

All rights reserved.

ISBN: **1522714781**
ISBN-13: **978-1522714781**

TABLE OF CONTENTS

ACKNOWLEDGMENTS	I
CHAPTER ONE	1
CHAPTER TWO	7
CHAPTER THREE	11
CHAPTER FOUR	17
CHAPTER FIVE	25
CHAPTER SIX	35
CHAPTER SEVEN	43
CHAPTER EIGHT	51
CHAPTER NINE	61
CHAPTER TEN	67
CHAPTER ELEVEN	73
CHAPTER TWELVE	81

CHAPTER THIRTEEN	87
CHAPTER FOURTEEN	93
CHAPTER FIFTEEN	101
CHAPTER SIXTEEN	109
CHAPTER SEVENTEEN	117
CHAPTER EIGHTEEN	123
CHAPTER NINETEEN	131
CHAPTER TWENTY	137
CHAPTER TWENTY-ONE	143
CHAPTER TWENTY-TWO	151
CHAPTER TWENTY-THREE	157
CHAPTER TWENTY-FOUR	165
CHAPTER TWENTY-FIVE	173
CHAPTER TWENTY-SIX	179
CHAPTER TWENTY-SEVEN	185

CHAPTER TWENTY-EIGHT	193
CHAPTER TWENTY-NINE	199
EPILOGUE	203
A LANCASTER COUNTY CHRISTMAS YULE GOAT CALAMITY	205
ABOUT THE AUTHOR	211

ACKNOWLEDGMENTS

All Praise first to the Almighty God who has given me this wonderful opportunity to share my words and stories with the world. Next, I have to thank my family, especially my husband Harold who supports me even when I am being extremely crabby. Further, I have to thank my wonderful friends and associates with Global Grafx Press who support me in every way as a writer. Lastly, I wouldn't be able to do any of this without you, my readers. I hold you in my heart and prayers and hope that you enjoy my books.

All the best and Blessings,

Ruth.

CHAPTER ONE

Jemima stood, watching and listening, at the property line of her family's farm. She leaned against the fence as Brad Williams clambered over, turned to kiss her one last time, and slowly melted into the darkness beyond. She stood listening as the crunch of his footsteps grew fainter and fainter, until the distant growl of a motor and the faint nimbus of unseen headlights flared, faded and disappeared.

After he had gone, the midnight world was very still and quiet. A solitary owl purred in the distance. Further still, a very faint sound: a train whistle from the crossing beyond town.

Jemima smiled, looked up into the starry sky and hugged herself.

It was turning cool, but the feel of Brad's mouth still tingled in her own, the warmth of his kisses was still on her lips, her face, her neck. She was trembling slightly. She had never in her life felt so alive. Jemima closed her eyes and replayed every word Brad had pressed into her ear. The way he'd said *duchess* this time made her look forward to hearing it again.

But best of all, better than anything, Brad Williams—the cynical, fast-talking reporter—had made himself completely, gloriously vulnerable.

He'd admitted that he loved her.

Jemima laughed suddenly, took her skirts in both hands and twirled around, making them billow out into the air like a blooming rose.

When she returned to the house, it was dark and still. There wasn't a light even in her parents' window, and the yard and the house were hushed. Jemima entered by the back porch. She opened the door softly, took off her shoes and crept up the back stairs, being careful not to make a sound.

The moon was as bright as day, slanting through the windows and hall floor. Jemima tiptoed past her parents' bedroom and the sound of her father's snores. She crept down the long hall, past Deborah's door. Jemima gave it a wary glance, but there was no light underneath it. Then she slowly twisted the knob to her own door, slid inside and closed it softly behind her.

Once she was safely inside, Jemima smiled and walked to the window. Under that dazzling moon she could see the whole countryside stretching out to the horizon. The dark trees were drawn in charcoal and the rolling hills in white chalk.

She unpinned her cap, unmade her bun and let her silken hair fall free. It cascaded over her hands, over her shoulders and past her waist in shining waves. She brushed it absently, and plaited it into a long braid.

Then she came out of her dress, letting it fall into a heap on the floor. She sat down on her bed, and unrolled her stockings, and tossed them away.

Jemima fell backward onto the bed and stared up at the moonlit ceiling, smiling. Against all odds, Brad Williams *loved* her.

She closed her eyes, savoring the memory. He'd *said* that he loved her. And it was true, she could *feel* it, she could *taste* it. He'd made himself vulnerable, he'd confessed his weakness against his own will. *Oh, Duchess* – the shuddering way he had said it, just before the insanity of those kisses – it was the cry of a man in love.

She knew it, she *knew* it, *she knew it.*

"Do you know what you do to me?" he had breathed into her ear. *"Do you know you make me lose my mind? I should never have come, I should have told you goodbye. This isn't right, it won't work, it will only make things harder in the end. I should leave..."*

But then he had kissed her like a madman, and pulled her

into his arms, and had lost his mind again. And after all the sweet insanity, after the Englischer's wild kisses, after her confusion and his despair, she was sure of only one thing:

Brad Williams might have lost his mind – but he wasn't leaving. He would be coming back, and back again, just as he'd done since the first day they met. Only this time, he wouldn't be after a story.

Jemima smiled again, and bit her nail, and dove under the covers.

The next morning Jemima was up bright and early, neat and trim and pressed. She hummed and smiled over her tasks as she helped make coffee and toast for breakfast. Her parents exchanged a knowing look.

Rachel came up behind her daughter, and slid an arm around her waist. "Well, *you* look happy this morning, Jemima!" she smiled, and kissed Jemima's cheek. "And I think I can guess why."

Deborah was sitting at the table and raised her brows and looked smug but said nothing.

Jemima received her mother's kiss and blushed. "I am, *very* happy," she agreed, and turned her attention to the coffee pot.

Rachel pursed her lips into a knowing smile. "I won't pry into your love life, Mima," she said primly, "but I expect you to tell your father and I *first* – if you have good news."

Deborah choked on her coffee and hacked horribly for a few minutes, but still emerged looking strangely amused. Jemima colored more deeply, and nodded to her mother and said nothing.

Jacob wiped his mouth with a napkin and added: "Well, now that all the nonsense is calming down at last, we can get back to normal. I'm going to clear the drive and put my anvils back in the shop, and about time."

Rachel set a plate of biscuits on the table and sat down next to Jacob. She looked at Jemima and added: "You'll be wanting to go to the bishop today, won't you, Jemima? You can make out a check to the community fund, and then you'll have the whole awful thing behind you."

She looked down mischievously, and smiled: "And certain *young men* will feel free to come calling, I expect."

Jemima sat down at the table and shook out a napkin. "I-I think I'd like to take a few weeks to just – just rest," she stammered. "I don't want to think about anything, right now. Everything has been so hard and – and *trying*."

Jacob looked at his eldest daughter sympathetically. "Yes, my poor girl, you *should* take a few weeks off to enjoy living like a teenager again," he told her. "This business has been more than an adult could've handled, much less a slip of a girl. You can take your time. Go to all the sings and frolics and games you please. Don't worry about the money, for now."

Rachel twitched her brows together, gave her husband a quick look and cleared her throat, but said nothing.

Jemima put a forkful of pancakes in her mouth, and was grateful for her parent's merciful attitude. But she also noticed, to her alarm, that Deborah's amused eyes still watched her all throughout the meal.

CHAPTER TWO

Jemima spent the following week like a hermit. She made no attempt to go out to games or frolics, or even the Sunday night sing. Jacob returned to his work and paid no heed to her seclusion, but Jemima could tell that her mother was puzzled, and a little worried. Rachel had asked no questions so far, but it was only a matter of time.

Jemima noticed her mother watching her at odd moments, and she could almost read the puzzled thought in her mind: *There's nothing standing in the way now. So why doesn't Jemima give the money away, so she can get married?*

It was a reasonable concern, and it was only a matter of time before her mother voiced it.

Jemima bent over her mending, pulling a needle through a torn quilt square. Her mother's warning came back to her: *"I don't know what you feel toward that boy, Mima. But I do know this: That boy is an Englischer. He lives in a different world. He thinks differently from you, he believes different things, and he wants different things. If you lose sight of that, you could be very bad hurt."*

She knew that her mother was right, but it was already too late. She'd lost sight of what she *should* do, or *should* say, or *should* feel. She'd lost sight of everything except what she *did* feel: the intoxication of Brad's lips on hers and of his arms around her.

There were a lot of things that were only a matter of time, and she knew she'd have to address them sooner or later: her mother's confusion, when to give the rest of the money away and what to do when Mark and Samuel and Joseph came to the house and started asking questions of their own.

Jemima pulled the thread taut and tied it off. The thought of hurting her friends was a painful one. She knew that sooner or later, she would have to look into Joseph's eyes, and Samuel's, and Mark's, and tell them what she had just learned herself: *I'm sorry, but I can't marry you. I'm in love with another man.* She couldn't allow herself to dwell on what that would do to them.

She couldn't allow herself to dwell on what she would do *herself*, when the magic faded and Brad inevitably returned to his own life. That, too, was far too painful a thought to dwell on; so she simply pushed it aside.

There would be a price to pay later, she knew. But she had made the decision to pay whatever it might cost her – her friendships, her reputation, her parents' approval. She had pushed the inevitable reckoning into the back of her mind.

All of those hard things were for later. Now, right now, she could only think of Brad.

She pulled her needle through the fabric. Brad had promised to come back on Saturday night, to their usual place. He had to commute all the way from the city to see her – almost fifty miles. It was a long way to travel.

But she was counting the days.

Jemima closed her eyes and leaned back into her chair. Instantly she was with Brad again under the stars. He had taken her hands and warmed them with his own.

"I'll be back again at the same time. Meet me here?"

Brad's blue eyes had glittered in his dark face. Those eyes had looked strange, otherworldly. The moon glanced off them and made them glow. It had been so like the dream she'd once had that it sent a shuddering thrill up her spine.

"Say you will, Duchess."

She'd whispered *yes*, and dug her fingers into his hair. Jemima smiled to herself. Brad's mop of hair was as thick as it looked; it was almost impenetrably dense, but surprisingly smooth and soft. She had dug her hands into that untamable hair, smoothed her hands down behind his ears and cupped them behind his neck.

He had taken her face in his hands and kissed her again, that last time – such a sweet, soft, *good night my love* kiss.

Jemima smiled, sighed and opened her eyes again.

It was only a few days until their next meeting. It was getting chilly at night now, so she'd decided to take a big quilt this time, to wrap around their shoulders. It would be snug and cozy. Maybe they could even sit on the porch swing, if he arrived late enough, after everyone was asleep. A little thermos of hot coffee might also be a nice welcome.

Of course it would be more comfortable indoors, and she toyed with the idea of bringing Brad inside the house, but rejected it as too risky. If her father came downstairs for any reason and saw her sitting there with the Englischer reporter, she trembled to think what he might do.

So for as long as they lasted, her meetings with Brad would have to remain a secret, known only to them.

Jemima's eyebrows twitched together. That is, if Deborah didn't betray them and bring the whole thing crashing down around their ears.

CHAPTER THREE

Jemima folded up the big quilt and carried it up to her bedroom, where she had also stashed a thermos and some cups. She had pushed the family picnic basket under her bed, to be ready when called for.

Jemima put a small finger to her lips, pondering. She couldn't decide if it would be better to have coffee or hot apple cider with caramel. She also planned to fill the basket with some cheese and fresh apples and crackers, and to make some coffee cake.

She reclined on the bed and closed her eyes. She could picture their next meeting already: the two of them snuggling together on the porch swing, toasty warm with the big quilt around them, and each of them warming their hands with a cup of piping hot cider.

And those weren't the *only* ways to stay warm on a chilly evening. Jemima smiled to herself and imagined Brad's arms, strong and tight around her.

A slight noise from the doorway made Jemima sit up suddenly. To her surprise and dismay, Deborah was standing there, eating a piece of pie and wearing an expression that hinted that she'd guessed *exactly* what her sister was thinking.

Deborah glanced back into the hall, and then leaned in through the doorway and drawled: "What's this you're working on – a big quilt? And you're hiding the picnic basket under your bed. Brad is coming back again, I see."

Jemima looked down and tried to assume a neutral expression, but she felt herself going hot with annoyance.

Deborah grinned at her and rolled her eyes to the ceiling in mock innocence. "A lookout *sure would* be handy, huh? You and Brad wouldn't have to worry about Daed coming down and catching you together."

Jemima stared at her grimly. "I don't know what you're talking about!"

Deborah sighed and crossed her arms. "*Sad*," she replied. "It's *sad* that you don't trust me, because I meant what I said. I could help you."

"This is a change for you, isn't it, Deborah?" she asked coolly. "You like to make fun of Joseph and Mark and Samuel, and of me when I talk to them. Why are you acting so different now?"

Deborah finished the piece of pie she was eating. "Because it isn't Joseph or Mark or Samuel this time," she replied, licking her fingers. "Your life is finally getting interesting – don't jinx it."

"I don't see why you're interested."

"I like Brad Williams. He's kind of cool. I think he'd be good for you," Deborah told her.

Jemima stared at her suspiciously, and Deborah shrugged. "Okay, that's not it. Or at least, not *all* of it. Maybe I *owe* him for something."

Jemima looked up sharply. "*Owe* him? What do you mean?"

"Oh, nothing serious," her sister replied. "Just that I made him pay me 50 dollars once, to bring you out to the garden."

"*What!*" Jemima cried, and stared at her younger sister in outrage. "Oh, Debby – tell me you're joking!"

Deborah nodded her head. "It's true."

"Why – how could you even *think* of such a thing!" Jemima gasped. "You have to give him his money back, right away!"

Deborah smiled, and shook her head. "No, I don't. Because he had it coming. He messed us *all* up. I was just making him pay for it, a little."

"*Of course* you have to give him his money back!" Jemima cried. "What he must think of us! Of all the dishonest, greedy—"

Deborah held up an admonishing finger. "Careful now, Mima. Remember what I know. You don't want me to change my mind about helping you. Right now, I'm willing, but that could change."

"*Oh!*" Jemima pinched her lips into a thin, straight line. "You should pray to God for forgiveness, *pray hard*! And now *I* have to pray that God will make me *willing* to forgive you – you little – you—"

Rachel walked down the hall behind them, and both Jemima and Deborah clamped their mouths shut and looked down at the floor. A few suspenseful seconds passed, and then their mother slowly returned.

Rachel poked her head into the doorway, and opened her mouth as if she was about to ask a question: but one look at Jemima's face made her turn her eyes from one of her daughters to the other.

"What's going on in here? Jemima, why do you look so – so *angry*? Is there something wrong?"

Deborah raised her brows significantly, and smiled.

Jemima bit her lip.

"No, nothing's wrong."

Rachel frowned, and looked from her to Deborah. "Are you sure? Deborah, what did you just say to your sister?"

Deborah regarded her with a kindling eye. "Why does everyone *always* think that if there's something wrong, it has to be *my* fault?" she demanded.

Jemima squeezed her eyes shut and prayed, but Deborah flounced out of the room, sparing her the necessity of a reply.

Rachel watched her go and turned her sympathetic eyes on her oldest daughter. "I don't know what just happened, but whatever it was, forgive your sister," she sighed.

"It's *so* hard, Mamm," Jemima murmured, and her mother nodded.

"I know, dear."

Her mother came over and kissed her, smiled, and put a calming hand to her cheek. Jemima looked up at her mother ruefully.

But after she left, Jemima squeezed her eyes together and stamped her foot on the floor. If it wasn't a sin, she could wish that Deborah would fly away to a desert island somewhere, where she would have to stay until she was thirty years old.

Or at least, old enough to know *not* to play so cruelly with other people's feelings.

Jemima shook her head bitterly. But in the meantime, it looked as if she was in Deborah's power. She could only pray that Deborah was willing to leave her in peace to enjoy what little time she had with Brad.

But given Deborah's actions so far, she had very little hope of it.

CHAPTER FOUR

When Saturday arrived, it dawned clear and crisp and cool under a cloudless blue sky. The rolling countryside around the King farm was as neat and trim as a postcard – white farmhouses, red barns, and green hills spattered with glorious color: fire red, copper orange, lemon yellow.

But Jemima hardly noticed the fine weather. She spent most of the day in the living room mending clothes, and the hours seemed to crawl. Every time she glanced at the old clock on the mantle, the hands seemed frozen to the same position they'd held the last time she looked.

The time dragged to noon. Jacob came in from his workshop, and they all ate lunch: thick slabs of bologna and homemade cheddar between Rachel's sourdough bread, homemade cream of chicken soup with baked butter crackers, a big bowl of potato salad with egg and dill, creamed corn, coffee and tea. Jacob and Rachel talked and laughed together, Deborah looked sour, and Jemima picked at her food, said little and glanced at the clock.

They finished lunch. Jacob kissed Rachel and went back to work. Jemima and Deborah helped their mother clear away the plates and glasses, and Jemima returned to the living room and went back to mending clothes and watching the clock.

A few more hours limped by. At five o'clock they all assembled again for dinner: meatloaf and gravy, biscuits, peas, pickled beets, more potatoes and apple pie with cheddar cheese on top. Jacob and Rachel talked and laughed together, Deborah looked sour, and Jemima picked at her food, remained mostly silent and watched the clock.

After dinner Jemima waited until her parents were occupied, then escaped upstairs. She ducked into the bathroom that she shared with Deborah and shut out the world.

Then she locked the door and ran a hot, fragrant bath.

When the tub was full of steaming water, Jemima peeled off her clothes, stepped gingerly into the hot water, and gradually eased herself into its enveloping warmth.

She sank down into the water until it had closed over her

ears like two hands. The radiant heat slowly drew all the tension and all the frustration of a long wait out of her.

She lathered her hands with a bar of soap until the suds were running through her fingers, then washed her hair and face and body. The soap was deliciously fragrant of honeysuckle, and the aroma filled the tiny room with the last whisper of summer.

Jemima luxuriated in the silky bubbles, breathed the perfume in deeply, and then rinsed it away with cool, clear water. She stepped out of the tub, dried herself, sat down on the edge and smoothed on honeysuckle lotion over her face and neck, all down her arms and legs, and her hands and feet. It felt silky smooth, and to Jemima's delight, the lotion made her skin as soft as a baby's.

After she had he wrapped herself in a bathrobe and her hair in a towel, Jemima slipped into her own room and stretched out on the bed to watch the sun go down through her windows.

The sky gradually melted from pale blue, to blue tinged with pink, to rose red, and then to lavender. Jemima watched it change with rising anticipation. When the sky outside her window deepened from lavender to indigo, she shook her luxurious hair out of the towel and brushed it to a high sheen. Then she pinned it into a coiling bun at the nape of her neck, and dressed in fresh clothes with more than her usual care.

She stood in front the mirror, pinned her cap in place, and

then stared at her own reflection. Her eyes looked dilated, her cheeks were flushed and her lips looked slightly swollen.

She turned to the window and looked out across the fields to the horizon. There was now only the faintest glow where the sun had been. The evening star burned high in the sky.

Behind the closed door, she could hear Deborah stump down the hall, shuffle into her own room and slam the door behind her. Farther away, she could hear the muffled sounds of her parent's voices, then the faint sound of their own door closing.

The sky deepened to dark blue and more stars began to glow here and there. All across the valley, Jemima watched as their neighbors' window lights winked out, one by one.

A deep quiet settled down over the house. The creaks and pops of an old house at night, and the sound of an owl calling outside sounded loud in the silence.

An hour passed…two hours…three. The sound of her father's snores wafted down the hall from her parent's bedroom. Jemima checked her bedside clock, walked to her bed and knelt down on the floor.

She pulled the picnic basket out and set it on the bed. She opened it, gave it one last check and saw that everything was neatly tucked inside. She closed it, locked it and folded the quilt on top of it.

Then she threw a shawl around her shoulders, pulled on

her stockings and shoes, picked up the basket and crept downstairs.

The air was sharp and chill when Jemima stepped out onto the porch. She hurried to the swing, draped the quilt over the seat back, and set the picnic basket down on the floor. Then she turned and took the now-familiar path to their meeting place.

There was only a crescent moon that night, and it was harder to see, but Jemima knew the way: across the lawn, across the bare, fallow ground that had been her mother's summer garden, through the thinning underbrush and on to the fence that divided their farm from the overgrown field next door.

There was little more than starlight, and Jemima leaned forward across the fence, peering out into the darkness. She saw nothing and heard nothing except the night sounds of small unseen animals somewhere in the field beyond – soft *chirps* and *clicks*.

Jemima turned her gaze to the road on the far side of the field. There were no visible lights.

She exhaled in disappointment, and rubbed her hands together under her shawl. The night was deepening, and it was cold.

A tiny sound off to the right made Jemima turn her head.

Suddenly a hand clamped over her mouth, and another

hand slid around her waist. Jemima uttered a smothered scream and rolled terrified eyes to a dark face hovering over her own.

The stranger yanked her to his chest and kissed her. But though she couldn't see his face, Jemima recognized the feel of Brad's kiss. She went limp with relief, then twisted to throw her arms around him.

"*You scared me to death*!" she gasped, but it was all she had time to say before he stopped her mouth with another fierce greeting.

Brad broke off and nuzzled her cheek. "I thought this week would never end! Oh, you smell so good," he murmured, and buried his face into her white neck.

Jemima rolled her eyes up and gasped. She was discovering that she loved the feel of Brad's lips on the tender skin just under her ear; she loved the way his lips teased their way down her neck – and set every spot on fire.

"Come to the house," she whispered, her eyes still closed. "Everyone is asleep, we can sit on the porch. I brought a big quilt, and food."

She slid her hand down his arm, found his hand and clasped it. "It's too cold out here. Come with me."

But he paid no attention. He kissed her again, mussed her hair and knocked her cap askew. Jemima put a distracted hand to her head. Hairpins were falling out everywhere, and now—

"*Oh, my hair—*" she cried softly. The shining skeins unraveled and fell to her waist like rivulets of water. Brad looked down momentarily, and captured one of the skeins with one hand and rubbed it between his fingers like silk.

Jemima took advantage of his momentary distraction. "Come with me, *come*. It's too cold out here."

Still he didn't move, so Jemima pulled out of his arms and, on a mischievous impulse, fled from him.

"*Duchess!*" His exasperated voice hissed out of the darkness, followed by sputtering laughter. "Where did you go? You know this isn't my—"

There was the sound of someone crashing into a bush, and stumbling footsteps. "*When I catch you—*"

Jemima laughed breathlessly, darted to him, grabbed his hand and pulled him across the garden plot and the lawn. He followed, laughing, and they ran up to the brink of the porch steps.

Jemima turned on him and caught him in her arms. "*Hissht! Be quiet, or my father will hear!*"

He stole another kiss before she pulled away again and led him up the steps and to the swing.

CHAPTER FIVE

Brad sat down on the swing and hurriedly wrapped the quilt around Jemima's shoulders, and then around his own.

"*Brrr*! It *is* cold!"

Jemima leaned down and opened up the picnic basket. "I have hot coffee," she told him, and opened the thermos. The scent of fresh-brewed roast curled up into the air.

"You're an angel," Brad told her gratefully, taking the hot cup between his hands. "*Mmmm.* Is that cake? I didn't have time for dinner, and I'm starving."

"Here, here," Jemima told him, and piled treats onto his plate: coffee cake, apple slices, cheese, dried apricots, a wedge of homemade fudge and a beef sandwich. She handed them to him, and he devoured them like a starving man.

Jemima sipped her coffee and watched him, smiling.

"This sure beats TV dinners," he told her, taking a big bite of the sandwich.

Jemima frowned. "Is that what you eat – TV dinners?" she cried. It wrung her heart to think of Brad sitting in his apartment alone, eating skimpy, tasteless portions off a cardboard plate.

He seemed oblivious to her dismay. "Mostly, unless I'm eating out. I'm not much of a cook."

"*Oh!*" Jemima leaned down and quickly made another plate, twice as big as the first. She handed it to Brad.

He took it, but asked: "Aren't you going to eat anything?"

"Oh, I had dinner long ago," she assured him. "Eat, *eat*! I hate to think of you driving for hours hungry!"

"I have to admit, this sure hits the spot," he replied, and made the coffee cake disappear, and all the other things, one by one. Then he leaned back into the swing, and closed his eyes and sighed deeply.

"There's more," Jemima told him, but he shook his head. He tilted his head, turned and stared at her without saying anything. He just sat there with an odd expression on his face, looking at her until she asked:

"*What?*"

For answer he reached out, and took two thick strands of her hair in his hands, and gently stretched them out, like shining ribbons. He wrapped his hands in them and brushed them across his cheek.

Jemima watched him in puzzlement. "What are you doing?" she whispered.

He smiled at her in the darkness. "I didn't know your hair was so *long*," he murmured, looking down at it. "It's beautiful. Soft as silk. I wish it was daylight, so I could see it better."

"If it were daylight, my hair would be pinned up, under my cap," she told him primly. "And we wouldn't be here."

He sighed heavily. "True enough. How do you—" He broke off abruptly.

Jemima tilted her head. "How do I what?" she asked gently.

"Nothing," he replied, but she persisted.

"How do I *bear it*, you mean? All the strict rules? Wearing the same thing every day, putting my hair up under a cap?"

"Look, I—"

"It's all right," she told him. "You're not the first person who's asked me that question. People don't understand. It's natural to be…curious."

"No, I'm sorry, Duchess. You have a perfect right to believe whatever you want. I'm a moron. I admit it." He leaned over, and kissed her apologetically.

Jemima received his apology willingly. His lips tasted of chocolate and apricots, and his arms were as warm as a woolen sweater. She smiled and touched her fingertip to his lip.

"You're not…what you said. You're smart, and you're kind. And I'm not angry."

He sighed, and rested his head lightly on her shoulder. "If I was smart or kind I wouldn't be here," he said, half to himself. "I'd leave you *alone*, Duchess. I'd let you find a husband who *understands*."

Jemima's eyes spangled with sudden tears. "Is that – is that what you *want?*" she cried. "Do you *want* me to marry Mark, or Sam—"

"*Of course not!*" He grabbed her suddenly, looked down at her with that crazy look in his eyes, and kissed her again so savagely that Jemima felt as if she were melting from every place that she touched him.

He buried his face in her neck. "I hate the thought of it!" he told her fiercely. "I *can't stand* to think of you with somebody else!"

Jemima laughed suddenly, and twined her arms around his neck. "Then I don't care," she told him. "That's all that matters. That you *love* me. And I don't want to talk about anything unhappy, not now. This is *our* time. Tell me – tell me about where you live."

"What?"

"*Yes* – tell me about where you live, and what furniture you have, and what pictures are on the wall. And what you read, and, and what you like to eat. All those things. And when you're gone, I'll imagine them in my mind, to help me pass the time until you come back."

He looked down at her, and sighed tenderly: "Oh, *Duchess*."

"Tell me."

He sighed again. "All right. I live in a studio apartment – oh, that means *small* – in the city. It is *not* as picturesque a neighborhood as yours. I think there's one tree in the parking lot, and it looks as if it's about to croak."

Jemima giggled into his chest, and he looked down at her, smiling. "Is that funny? Yeah, I guess it is. So, there's the croaking tree, and the complex is next door to a fast food place on one side and a pipe shop on the other."

Jemima looked up at him innocently. "What's a pipe shop?"

Brad ran a hand through his hair. "*Ah* – it's a place where – where people buy *–pipes.*"

"Oh."

"I'm on the second floor," he hastened to add, "and my unit's at the end of the row, which is good, because I only share one wall with a neighbor."

"Who is your neighbor?" Jemima asked, looking up at him.

"A guy from Guatemala. He's pretty laid back, but we don't talk much, because I usually come in la— I mean, I don't – don't see much of him."

"Oh."

"My furniture is mostly stuff I bought in a box and assembled. Though I did score a World War I office desk at a yard sale last year. I have a bookshelf crammed with sci-fi and history. I also have a good bit of biography – Disraeli, Lincoln, Eleanor Roosevelt, Einstein, Tesla. I like reading about real people."

Jemima nodded earnestly.

"And as for what's on my walls – I have some posters, mostly groups – I'm into roots music, blues, bluegrass – so mostly obscure stuff. And I don't cook much of anything. I do takeout when I'm tired, and stuff I can microwave when I'm not."

Jemima reached out and caressed his cheek

sympathetically. "You don't eat well, I can see it," she murmured sympathetically. "I'll pack some things for you to take home for tomorrow."

Brad cracked a grin. "*Worried* about me, are you, Duchess?"

She ran her fingers lightly over his bruised chin. "You *know* I—"

But she was cut off with shocking suddenness. The screen door flew open, and they both jumped to their feet in alarm, but it was Deborah's face that peeked out from behind the door.

"*Hide, quick! Daed is coming downstairs!*" she hissed, and darted back inside.

Jemima grabbed up the picnic basket and blanket, and took Brad's hand. They fled down the porch steps and stopped just at the corner of the house, listening.

A light bloomed in the window overhead and gave off a faint yellow glow.

Jacob's voice grumbled: "Deborah – what are you doing down here so early?"

Deborah piped, "Oh, I was hungry, I wanted a snack."

"Is that why I smell coffee?"

Jemima put a hand to her mouth and looked up at Brad in

dismay.

Deborah's voice sounded uncertain, but she answered: "Umm…yes. I got some leftover coffee from dinner."

The floorboards groaned under Jacob's massive footsteps. "How did you heat it without lighting the stove?"

"Ah – it's the *grounds* you smell. I opened the can, but I changed my mind and drank the cold leftovers." There was a quick, rummaging sound. "Do you want me to light the stove now?"

"No, no. There are still hours to sunrise. Eat and go back to bed."

"Why are *you* up so early, Daed?" Deborah queried.

The floorboards groaned again under the sound of heavy footsteps, and to Jemima's dismay, the screen door creaked open.

"I heard a noise and thought I'd check. If I catch one more *verruckt* Englischer sneaking around this house, I'll send him to the blessed God, no matter what your mother says."

Jemima pressed Brad's hand, and looked up at him, but his face was in shadow.

"Oh, now, Daed!" Deborah laughed unconvincingly. "It was only *me*, coming down to the kitchen. Want a piece of pie?"

The screen door closed again. "Just a little piece, and then back to bed, for both of us."

A few more minutes passed, and Jemima held Brad's hand tight. Then the light faded out, and heavy footsteps rang out again, then faded.

When it was silent and dark again, Jemima went limp against Brad's chest, and then lifted her face.

"*You should go. He might come back.*"

He leaned down, found her lips and kissed her. "*When can I see you again?*"

"Sunday night, next time. I'll meet you at the same place, and the same time." She pressed the basket into his hands. "*Take this home with you.*"

"*I can't take this whole….*"

"*Yes, yes.*" She leaned into him, kissed him, pressed her hand over his, and she could feel him relent.

"*All right then, Duchess. I'll bring it back next time, only it'll be my treat then. Deal?*"

"*Just so long as you come back,*" Jemima breathed, twined her hands around the back of his neck, and pulled him to her lips. She poured all her love into that goodbye kiss, all her longing, and was gratified to hear him gasp when their lips parted.

"You shouldn't kiss me like that if you want me to go," he warned.

Jemima instantly replied: *"I don't want you to go!"*

Brad dropped the basket and gave her a lengthy and very communicative kiss in reply. Then he turned away, turned back to give her one more for good measure, and disappeared into the general darkness.

Jemima stared after him for a long time before the pinching cold finally made her give up, and turn to seek her own bed.

CHAPTER SIX

Jemima moaned and turned her face into her pillow. "*Kiss me, Brad!*" she murmured. But instead of Brad placing a tender kiss on her lips, an impatient hand shook her shoulder roughly. She opened her eyes, frowning.

The sky outside was still dark; the glow of a single candle provided the only light in the room. Gradually the dark blob hovering over her resolved into a human face. Deborah held a candlestick high overhead, and leered down at her.

"*'Kiss me, Brad*!'" she simpered. "You'd better be glad it's *me* who's waking you up, and not Mamm!"

"What's the matter? What is it?" Jemima cried, her mind

still clouded by dreams.

"What is it? It's almost *five,* lady of leisure, and Mamm says that if you don't get up, she's going to come and drag you out of bed by your feet. You've overslept!"

"*Oh!*"

Deborah shook her head and left, but Jemima scrambled out of bed, searching for her clothes. If only they'd let her sleep in, just once! She'd been dreaming the loveliest dream that she was in Brad's arms and that he was just about to ask her…

"*JeMIMa!*"

Jemima put a hand to her mouth. Her father hadn't used that tone of voice to her in *years.*

"Coming!" she cried, and hurried to put her hair up and dress.

It was Sunday, and they were going to worship at Silas Fisher's, so breakfast was somewhat hurried. Jemima was present in body only, and performed only the bare minimum required of her: a brief *yes, no,* or nod of the head, when she was directly addressed. She had no memory of the meal, or what anyone said – she could only think of Brad.

On the buggy ride to the Fisher farm, Jemima looked out across the fields to the horizon, but what she was seeing was a cramped studio apartment in the city with one tall, bright-eyed occupant. She saw him open the door clumsily in the wee hours of the morning, carrying a big picnic basket on one arm. She saw him set it on the breakfast counter, walk a few big paces across the room, and collapse on a narrow bed pushed up against one wall.

Poor Brad!

She frowned, wishing there was some way she could meet him halfway, instead of him having to make such a long trip at night. But she had no transportation…

"*Jemima!*"

She looked up, startled. Her mother had half-turned and was looking at her in exasperation from the front seat of the buggy. "What did I just say to you?"

Jemima gaped at her in dismay. "Oh…I…"

Deborah rolled her eyes. "Oh, never mind her, Mamm. She's mooning over her boyfriends," she put in unexpectedly. "She's been worthless for *days*."

Jemima gave her sister a glance that was expressive of gratitude – and surprise.

Rachel pursed her lips in exasperation. "Jemima, I asked you if you remembered to bring the book I promised to loan your Aunt Priscilla."

Jemima stared at her guiltily.

"Well – *did* you?"

"No...no, I'm sorry...I forgot."

Her mother looked at her in exasperation. "Child, what will I do with you?" she wailed softly. "But I suppose all young girls are a little distracted when they're..." she bit her lip, smiled faintly and turned back around.

Jemima watched her mother with worried eyes, and then turned to look at her sister. Deborah had saved her last night, and even this morning she was helping her to deflect suspicion. Was it possible that for once in her life, Deborah was trying to be *helpful*?

Deborah felt her gaze, turned and winked at her. Jemima frowned, turned back to her contemplation of the countryside, and remained silent for the rest of the drive.

The Fisher farm was a sprawling complex of four big houses, six barns, and a dozen other outbuildings clustered at the center of acres of corn and wheat. The weather was overcast and cold, but it did not seem likely to rain, so helpers had set up worship benches inside the main barn, and on the lawn outside.

Jacob parked the buggy next to dozens of others lined up on the grass, and they walked down the long road. Jemima kept her eyes on her feet, because she was suddenly stabbed by the fear that Joseph or Mark or Samuel would find her – and she had nothing to give them but heartache.

Jemima followed her mother and Deborah to the main barn, where worship was being held, and sat beside them on the women's benches. She was careful to move to the very end of the row, where she could hide behind Dorcas Hershberger. According to the local grapevine, Dorcas weighed 250 pounds at least. In any case she made an excellent screen; behind her, Jemima didn't have to worry about looking up, and seeing a boy's eyes pleading with her.

As the long, slow hymn singing began, Jemima retreated inside her own mind. It helped her stave off her growing fear that she'd jumped the fence, that she'd strayed into uncharted and dangerous territory.

Jemima gnawed her fingernail. She'd never met anyone who'd gone out with an Englischer – much less fallen in love with one. It just wasn't done.

So what would happen, now that she *had* fallen in love with one?

She closed her eyes. *Hurt.* Yes, a lot of hurt for everyone involved. Pain for her when she had to tell her suitors that she couldn't marry them. Pain for them, because they all loved her. Pain for her parents when their dreams for her didn't come true.

Pain for her and for Brad when they had to part ways at last – because there was no realistic future for the two of them.

Pain for her again, after, when no one else could *ever* be Brad Williams.

Her Mamm had been right: she was going to hurt badly, she was going to hurt other people. The smart thing, the best thing, would be to forget Brad, choose a husband and settle down.

But if she did, which one of them – and how could she choose?

Dorcas Hershberger suddenly leaned down to get something she'd dropped, and for a second Jemima had a clear view of the men's worship benches. Instantly she was aware that three pairs of eyes were looking at her. Jemima's guilty gaze moved from Joseph's hopeful face, to Samuel's questioning glance, to Mark's sad and steady eyes on her.

She felt tears coming to the surface again, and dropped her glance. *No, she couldn't do it.* It would be mean and dishonest to marry Joseph or Samuel or Mark when she was really only *fond* of them. It would be cruel to let one of them pour his whole life into a fantasy.

Because sooner or later, he'd see the truth – and hate her for it.

No, whatever she had to face, it was better to face it and have done. Better to wound a friend honestly, than to poison his whole life with a lie.

Tears sparkled in Jemima's eyes. *Oh Lord*, she prayed, *I*

know I'm not supposed to love an Englisch boy. But please, even if I am doing wrong, help me to tell Mark and Joseph and Samuel what I must. Please comfort them – they're going to be hurt.

Please don't let them hate me for it. I do still love them so!

CHAPTER SEVEN

After worship, Jemima went directly to the Fisher kitchen to help the other girls serve lunch. It was the way things had always been done, and on this particular Sunday, Jemima was glad of the tradition.

She took a platter of pickled beets off the counter, because she knew that Mark and Joseph and Samuel all hated them. She was on the brink of tears and didn't trust herself to face her suitors with equanimity.

When she emerged from the house, Jemima quickly sized up the seating arrangement on the lawn, but to her dismay, her suitors had foiled her. She had hoped to hide in a safe corner, but Joseph was to the left, Samuel was seated in the middle, and Mark was to the right. No matter where she went, *one* of them would be there.

But to Jemima's surprise, Deborah appeared at her elbow, carrying a platter of sandwiches. She turned her head slightly and whispered: *"Don't worry, I'll come with you."*

Jemima couldn't help glancing at her sister in astonishment, but Deborah's freckled face was as placid as dawn. She leaned over again.

"Let's get it over with."

Jemima nodded, and walked down the porch steps. She walked past each table, serving whenever asked. She kept her gaze strictly on the table, spoke only when she was greeted, and answered with a demure smile and downturned eyes.

Her heart began to beat oddly when she approached Joseph's table. She'd never had the chance to talk to Joseph. He still considered them engaged because he'd kissed her one evening. Never mind that it was completely his own idea, and that she'd denied it. *He* believed it, and that was the important thing.

Jemima felt her face going warm, and kept her eyes on the tablecloth as she served the food. But to her dismay, she heard Joseph's voice calling her.

"Good morning, Jemima," he called softly. "Would you give me some beets, too?"

She nodded, but didn't look up. She moved around the table to Joseph's chair, and to her dismay, as she extended her arm to serve him, Joseph surreptitiously slid a small, folded piece of paper up her sleeve.

Jemima lifted her arm at once to keep the paper from falling out on the table in front of everyone, went beet red herself and scrambled to keep the platter from overturning.

"Thank you, Jemima," Joseph murmured, and brushed her sleeve fleetingly with his hand.

Jemima fled back to the house, holding one arm up to keep the paper from falling out onto the ground. She slapped the platter on a countertop, slipped past the other girls lined up outside the kitchen, and found an empty bathroom to hide in. She ducked inside and locked the door behind her, then leaned against it with her eyes closed.

After she had gathered her nerve, Jemima lowered her sleeve and let the paper fall out into her palm. She unfolded it and read:

My maus,

I have heard almost nothing from you in the last few weeks and have missed you very much. Have you given the last of the money away? I will be happy when you do. I am anxious to announce our engagement. I want everyone to know that you are my fiancée!

Jemima put a hand to her mouth and squeezed her eyes

shut to prevent herself from crying.

I have my eye on a house near my brother's farm, for the two of us. I will take you to see it as soon as your business with the money is over. It is small now, but I can add more rooms as we need them.

Jemima shook her head, and choked off a sob. *Poor Joseph!*

When she had calmed down again, she tore the note into tiny pieces and threw it into the trashcan. She couldn't let someone else find it and read it, and nothing poor Joseph said was going to make a difference now, anyway.

Jemima leaned over the sink and splashed her face with cool water. She couldn't afford to advertise that she was upset, not with so many eyes looking at her. She splashed her face again.

After a few minutes her eyes looked more normal, and she had regained a calm expression by sheer will power. She told her reflection that she was going to talk to Joseph, but that *time* and *place* were important, that absolute *privacy* was important and she couldn't bear to do it *now*.

Jemima took a deep breath, smoothed out her skirts, opened the door and walked out again.

But as soon as she had set foot into the little hall outside, something grabbed her and swirled her through the doorway of a neighboring room. She had no sooner recognized the dark blur as Samuel, than he pulled her into his arms and kissed her.

Jemima pulled back from him and turned her face away, blushing. "*Samuel!* What a way to behave – at worship, too!"

He reached for her again. "I've missed you! You've been away for so long, I was afraid you were sick."

Jemima looked down at the floor. "No, no – I haven't been sick," she stammered. "I just needed to, to *rest*, after all the awful things that have happened." She looked up into his face. "I *still* need to rest, Samuel."

His expressive blue eyes registered pity, and then tenderness. "Yes, it has been hard on you, Mima," he agreed, flicking a wisp of her hair with his fingertip. "I'm sorry if I came on too strong, but I just had to see you again. And – I'm still waiting for an answer to my question."

Jemima looked away. She couldn't bear to meet Samuel's eyes, because now they were radiating feelings that she couldn't return. She raised the only objection she could afford to confess.

"I know, Samuel. I *know*. But I still have things to do," she stammered. "I still have so much of the money left."

"When are you planning to give it away, Mima?" Samuel asked, frowning slightly. "I don't mean to pry, but I-I would've thought—"

Jemima bit her lip. "There have been so many other things to do, I haven't had time, Samuel," she replied, and then blushed to think that she'd lied. "I do mean to give it away. I *will*."

Samuel went silent, and Jemima prayed for some distraction to break the awkward silence. And it seemed that God had pity on her, because just then, Deborah's strident voice echoed from the hall outside:

"*Mima*! Where are you? Mamm wants you."

Jemima breathed a prayer of thanks, and looked up apologetically into Samuel's puzzled face. "Oh, I'm sorry, Samuel," she murmured, "I have to go."

"Think about what I said, Mima," he urged, and clasped her hands.

"I will, Samuel, I promise," Jemima told him – and fled.

As soon as she was well away, Jemima gripped Deborah's wrist and pulled her into a little anteroom, away from the sound of voices.

Jemima glared down into her sister's startled eyes. "I want you to tell Mamm that you're feeling sick," she whispered fiercely. "Tell her that you're bad sick to your stomach, that we have to go home. If I don't get out of here now, I'm going to break down. Do you understand? I might not make it even now!"

Jemima's angry façade crumbled suddenly. She put a hand to her mouth to stifle a sob.

Deborah nodded. "All right, I will. We'll go back to the buggy, but we'll have to go out the back way, through the trees. We'd better keep out of sight, or you might get waylaid again."

They escaped out the back door, hurried through the yard, and walked to the buggies behind a long line of thick fir trees that mostly screened them from view.

When they had reached the safety of the buggy, and Jemima was hidden away inside, Deborah looked up into her face and said: "Stay here, I'll bring Mamm and Daed back to you. And try not to bust out crying, will you? It'll make my job easier."

Jemima nodded, and watched her sister disappear into the bushes again. She hugged her knees, and rocked back and forth, and tried to concentrate on her blessings.

But the thing she was most grateful for at the moment, was that her sly, tricky sister was on her side – for *once*.

CHAPTER EIGHT

Although Deborah had helped her escape from her suitors, Jemima soon regretted asking her for help. Because Deborah's help always came with a price tag.

No sooner had they gotten home, than Deborah turned the situation to her advantage. She announced to her startled family that she was *seriously* ill.

"I have to lie *down*," Deborah groaned dramatically. "I feel so *sick*!"

Deborah languished on the living room couch for the rest of that day. To Jemima's surprise and indignation, Deborah's mysterious illness hung on through the next day, and the next.

Deborah told their parents that she was too ill to do any work.

Which meant that Jemima was forced to do both Deborah's chores, and her own. To make things worse, Deborah made Jemima fetch and carry for her like a maid. Jemima grumbled under her breath, but she couldn't very well accuse Deborah, because *she* was the one who'd asked her sister to lie in the first place.

Deborah proved to be extremely fond of a soft couch, and was a frighteningly good liar. When their parents were in the room, Deborah moaned, and rolled her head back and forth on her pillow, and was seemingly racked by spasms of uncontrollable nausea. But after they left, she sat up and laughed wickedly.

She sprinkled water on her face and nightgown to simulate perspiration, she complained constantly of spinning vertigo, and she refused all but the blandest foods.

But when their parents were gone, she made Jemima go to the kitchen and bring up a plate of all of her favorite treats to eat on the sly.

By midweek, Jemima was so heartily sick of this performance that she considered making a confession to her parents; but she was spared the necessity. Whether because she sensed Jemima's rebellion, or because she herself was tired of the charade, Deborah suddenly declared herself much improved and hinted that she could probably eat – if she was fed.

Fortified with all her favorite foods, Deborah recovered from her illness with amazing speed, and started doing her own chores again. Life settled back into its familiar routine, but Jemima decided not to scold her sister.

She didn't have time to quarrel with her, because Brad would return on Sunday night, and she had no room in her heart for anything else.

The remaining days passed slowly. To Jemima, they seemed like years, and she could hardly contain her impatience – but Sunday night arrived at last.

It was a crisp, cold October night, bare of leaves – the wind had stripped the branches of every tree, and even the bushes were mostly bare. The landscape was washed by the light of a full moon, and every star glittered with a sharp, chill brilliance; but, off to the west, clouds scudded across the horizon, and the feel of snow was in the air.

Jemima waited in her bedroom, watching the clock by the light of a single candle. The night was cold, but she had two thick quilts to nestle in, and she had hot cider and coffee in two thermos jugs.

She had also taken the precaution of enlisting Deborah's help. She was reasonably sure, now, that Deborah wouldn't betray them.

She opened her door, crossed the hall, and rapped softly on Deborah's door. It opened, and Deborah's sly face appeared in the crack.

"*Time*," Jemima whispered.

Her door opened, and Jemima gave her a quilt and a thermos to carry. "*Be quiet,*" she warned, and they descended the front stairs as softly as they could.

Deborah sat down on the couch in the living room to serve as lookout, and Jemima walked out onto the porch.

She breathed in the cold air. It tasted like ice from a silver cup, but the moon was bright and would help Brad find his way. She walked quietly to the swing, arranged the quilts, and set the thermos jugs on the floor. Then she skipped down the porch steps and crossed the lawn.

She could see Brad as soon as she rounded the corner of the house; he was walking across the garden in the moonlight with the picnic basket in one hand. Jemima smiled and ran to meet him.

The shadow stooped, set down the basket, and held its arms wide.

Jemima jumped into them, and two strong arms closed around her, lifted her feet off the ground and spun her through the air.

She buried her face in Brad's shoulder and laughed breathlessly: "*Stop, stop! My head is spinning!*"

But he had no mercy, because no sooner were her feet back

on the ground than he kissed her, braced her back, and bent her away from him until she seemed to be floating out over the ground. She looked up, and could see the stars, winking high overhead. Then he kissed her, and slowly raised her up again. She leaned against his chest, laughing.

"Are you hungry?" he teased her.

She nodded, and he took her hand. "Come on then. I have a basket full of Thai food. You're going to love it."

They ran across the lawn, laughing breathlessly, and stopped just short of the porch. Jemima put her hand on his chest and lifted a finger to her lips.

"*Careful! Remember last time,*" she breathed.

They walked quietly across the porch and settled into the swing. Brad set a small dark lantern on the floor, and a small puddle of light appeared at their feet. Brad knelt down and opened the basket lid. A delicious aroma rose heavenward.

He looked up at her. "Have you ever had Thai food before?"

Jemima shook her head.

"You'll love it. This is courtesy of the little storefront restaurant across the street from my complex. The cook there is an artist."

He lifted the lid off a covered dish, and a fragrant perfume rose up. "Try the cashew chicken. It's amazing." He rummaged in the basket for a cup, a fork and a napkin, and gave them to Jemima with a flourish.

She giggled, and took an experimental forkful. The flavors were unlike anything she was used to – they were spicy and creamy and nutty and sweet, all at once.

It was *delicious*.

She closed her eyes and rolled it luxuriantly in her mouth. When she opened her eyes again, she was embarrassed to find Brad smiling at her, because she had been making involuntary *mmm* sounds. She lowered her eyes in embarrassment but Brad only laughed.

"I told you," he grinned. "Here, have some of mine. This is called pad thai." He held out a heaping forkful of some noodle concoction, and placed it carefully into her mouth. Jemima closed her lips over it and savored the taste.

"*Um Bwad*," she murmured, "*se gud!*"

He found the coffee thermos, poured out two cups and gave one to Jemima. She took it gratefully and gingerly sipped it. The heat from the drink was a welcome relief from the cold.

Brad settled into the swing beside her and began to eat. Jemima watched him, but then cried, "Oh, we forgot!"

He turned to her. "Forgot what?"

"*Grace*," Jemima told him firmly, and bowed her head in

silence. Brad watched her, and waited politely until she raised her head again.

"You don't say grace before you eat?" Jemima asked innocently.

Brad shook his head. "No. I'm an agnostic."

Jemima took another forkful of chicken and ate thoughtfully before replying: "What's an *agnostic*?"

Brad smiled at her and shook his head. "It means I acknowledge that there *might* be a God, but I'm not sure of it."

"Oh."

"Maybe if I'd had a different childhood, I might've," he sighed. "But it's hard to believe in God when your Dad skips out and your Mom is a meth freak." He broke off, and shook his head. "That's all. Maybe there is a God, and He just isn't involved. I don't know."

They ate in silence for a few minutes, and Brad turned to her again and took her hand. "Look, Duchess, the religion thing doesn't matter to me. I don't care what you believe, or if you believe in anything. But – I know it's important to *you*."

He fell silent and looked down. "*How* important is it, Jemima? Could you – ever consider, say – moving away from home, and living somewhere else? Maybe not even being

Amish anymore?"

Jemima looked up at him sharply. "Oh, Brad, don't ask me," she whispered. "I couldn't. I *couldn't,* that's all."

He didn't raise his head. "Is that because of your religion, Duchess, or is it because of one of those guys you told me about? The ones who want to marry you? Have you made up your mind about *them*?"

Jemima fell silent. She looked down at her lap. "I'm not going to marry any of them," she whispered.

Brad nodded. "Why *not*?"

Jemima stared steadfastly at her hands. A wave of shyness washed over her. The silence stretched out.

"Because—"

She closed her eyes and tried again.

"Because I—"

She turned to him suddenly, impatient with herself, and took his face in her hands and kissed him like she had never kissed any boy in her life. She meant the kiss to communicate what she *felt* but could not *say*; but, to her surprise, Brad took her hands in his and pulled back from her lips.

"No, Duchess," he whispered, looking into her eyes. "I know you like to kiss me. What I don't know is *why*."

Jemima gasped. She was pierced by the guilty insight –

Brad was right. She wasn't being fair to him. In fact, she was doing the *very same thing* to him that Mark and Samuel and Joseph had done to *her*.

Jemima nodded, leaned forward and met his eyes.

"I can't marry them," she whispered, "because I'm in love with another man."

Brad's voice was barely audible. "Lucky guy. Anyone I know?"

Jemima laughed suddenly and rested her brow against his. "Silly! You know."

"Say it," he murmured. "*Say* it, Duchess."

"I love you," she breathed, "I love you, I love you, I *love*—"

But that was as far as she got.

CHAPTER NINE

Brad Williams made the long drive back to the city in the wee hours of Monday morning. It was a challenging drive. The Amish farmland was inked out in a way that only remote countryside can be: there were no street lights and no house lights. There was only the faint glow of his dashboard dials and the headlights of the truck. His headlights suddenly flushed out a deer, and he got a glimpse of a startled buck before the animal bounded across the dirt road, and away.

Overhead, the moon bathed the hills and fields with a ghostly luminescence, and the sky was awash with stars. They seemed sharper and clearer because of the cold, and to Brad, they seemed to smile.

He lit a cigarette, inhaled, and let the smoke curl through the cold air. The Duchess had said that she loved him. He still couldn't believe it.

He cracked a grin. Maybe there *was* a God after all!

He slowed the truck to a crawl and carefully crossed the narrow wooden bridge that spanned the river. The wooden planks made a hollow sound as the truck tires rolled over.

He stopped the truck and turned onto Yoder Road, the paved two-lane that would take him to town. A few ancient-looking street lights made anemic gray puddles here and there.

But he cruised slowly over the deserted road. He wanted to remember what the sleeping fields and darkened town looked like on this *magical* night.

He closed his eyes briefly and relived the passionate kiss the Duchess had given him. He replayed the sound of her melting voice whispering *I love you.*

In the moonlight she had looked almost supernaturally beautiful, like a nymph from some ancient myth. Even the darkness couldn't defeat the preternatural loveliness of those eyes; they had sparkled an icy green, even in the faint light of the moon.

Her lips were like wet velvet, and the sweet things they'd said to him were beyond fantasy. No other girl's kiss had ever sent such an electric sensation crawling up his spine; no other girl's words of love had destroyed and delighted him like hers.

He inhaled deeply from the cigarette, closed his eyes and exhaled slowly.

He was a *very* lucky man.

He opened his eyes again and pulled the truck to a stop. He was now at the one and only red light in downtown Serenity. The streetlights bathed the old brick storefronts in an unearthly orange glow, and all the buildings were blank-faced and locked up tight. There were still two hours between him and his bed. But he would've made the trip a thousand times over to hear and feel what he'd experienced this night.

He nudged the gas pedal, and the truck rolled slowly through the deserted town square. At the stop sign beyond, Brad turned left onto another paved two-lane – the one that eventually funneled into the highway.

He picked up a little speed over the empty road. Of course, there was the *religion* thing, but he hadn't expected Jemima to toss a lifetime of indoctrination over her shoulder in one night. He breathed out smoke and adjusted the heat vent.

But if he kept talking to her, and gave her a chance to see what she was missing, he was reasonably sure that he could get her to leave the green hill country and join the world. Eventually.

Or at least, he *hoped* he could.

He imagined waking up every morning to Jemima's gentle voice whispering in his ear. He closed his eyes briefly.

Good morning tiger, her dulcet voice purred. Jemima's slanting green eyes smiled at him over the bed sheet. One silky leg rubbed sensuously against his.

I never knew it could be like this, she whispered, and then bit his ear, very gently.

A car horn blared and dazzling lights swept across the front of the truck. Brad cursed and yanked the wheel. The oncoming car missed him by inches and disappeared into the night.

He had drifted over the yellow line.

Brad stared wide-eyed at the road, panting and his heart racing. He cursed himself for a fool and gripped the wheel.

But five minutes later, he was dreaming again.

By some miracle, Brad arrived at his own door hours later, at 2 in the morning. He fumbled with the keys, swung the door open, stumbled in and locked the door behind him.

Then he shuffled across the floor to his bedroom, shedding his clothes along the way, and fell back across the mattress.

He stared up at the ceiling. Jemima's angel face smiled down at him and murmured, *I love you, Brad.*

The Duchess *loved* him. He smiled, stretched out his arms,

and crossed them behind his head.

He'd aced those Amish guys, all *three* of them. It was like winning the World Series on the other team's field.

But he was still 50 long miles away, and those guys were right there with her, every day. They lived practically on Jemima's doorstep, and they were all hot to marry her. If he didn't step up fast, *one* of them was sure to move in on the Duchess.

Brad's smile faded, imagining it. He hadn't known he was capable of violent jealousy, but the thought of Jemima in some *other* guy's arms made him think *extremely* uncivilized thoughts.

He needed to make his move. In fact, the sooner he got Jemima *out* of there, the better.

And so, he was back to her religion again. *That* was why she still wanted to stay. *That* was the only obstacle left. How to overcome it?

He turned the problem over in his mind. If he started nagging the Duchess to change her beliefs, she'd probably get mad. No, that would be clumsy and was likely to end badly.

But she might respond if he framed it in a different way. He could promise to learn about *her* religion, provided she agreed to learn about the *Englisch* world.

If he could get her away from the green hill country, and

out into the real world, she'd see that her religion was holding her back. She'd see that modern life was *so* much better than a life of needless hardships and absurd restrictions.

He could show her how much fun living in the Englisch world could be. And then – oh, *baby*.

Brad grinned a sharp, white, ear-to-ear grin, sighed and closed his eyes.

CHAPTER TEN

At noon the next day, Delores Watkins sauntered up behind Brad William's desk chair and glanced at his computer screen. Her eyebrows arched up, but she held her peace.

An instant later Brad sensed her there, and colored to the roots of his hair. He swiveled the chair around and gave her a sheepish grin. "Ah – Delores! I didn't see you there! What can I do for you?"

Delores swept him with her heavy lashes and smiled indulgently. "Don't worry, lover boy," she assured him. "I won't tell anyone that you shop at"—she adjusted her glasses—"*Angel Secrets*. Though I confess—"

"Cut to the chase, Delores," Brad interrupted evenly. "This is my lunch break."

"Yes, you're finally awake! Your bleary mornings are beginning to make sense to me now. I don't object to romance, Brad, but if yours is *newsworthy*, throw the *Ledger* a bone – promise?"

She tossed a report down on his desk, winked at him, laughed at his expression and surged away, like some massive ship.

Brad watched her go grimly, and turned back to his task – but not before closing his office door, to prevent any further intrusions.

He sat down in front of the computer and returned to the *Angel Secrets* gift page. He clicked on a series of lovely, frilly things, the sort of frou-frous all women everywhere loved, and– he'd be willing to bet – even *Amish* women dreamed of, in their weaker moments.

And *weak* was what he was shooting for.

Seduction.

The jewelry page displayed a tiny, elfin gold ring with one delicate emerald chip. It would match the Duchess' eyes to perfection. He clicked on it.

The next page showed a pair of tiny hair barrettes covered in pink, feathery fuzz. Brad lingered over them, fantasizing about what it would feel like to set them in Jemima's flowing hair. He clicked on them, too.

Later on, there were little bottles of perfume, scented soaps and flavored lip gloss with names like *'50s Magnolia, Champagne Ice Cream,* and *Winged Fantasy.* Brad chose a small, exquisite vial of a perfume called *Moonlight Angel.* It was a tiny bottle of cobalt blue glass bearing a blue-and-gold foil label. A tiny gold fringe hung from the bottle neck. He clicked on it, too.

It was the first phase of his campaign to win Jemima away from his last, daunting rival: the Amish church.

He'd start with little gifts of the kind that all girls loved. It would be an innocent gesture, one that men in love were supposed to make – but, hopefully, it would do more than just touch Jemima's heart.

He hoped that it would open her eyes – just a little – to what she was missing. He was confident that, sooner or later, nature would kick in.

It was against nature for a beautiful girl like Jemima to wear drab clothing every day of her life. She should be free to revel in her youth and beauty and enjoy sweet nonsense like—he looked down at the screen—bubble gum lip gloss, and pink nail polish, and even *more* delightfully girly gifts that he was not yet bold enough to give her.

But totally planned to in the near future.

He smiled, imagining Jemima's delight when he presented these frilly nothings. It would probably be the first time she'd ever been given a remotely lover-like gift, and it was going to be fun to watch her face when she opened them up.

He leaned back in his chair and crossed his arms over his head. That Amish asceticism made him kind of *mad*, really – the Duchess was 18 years old, an adult, and had never in her life worn lip gloss, or jewelry or even pretty barrettes in her hair. It was a kind of abuse to make a beautiful girl feel bad about such harmless pleasures – the pretty things that *should* be a beauty's birthright.

Well, he intended to change all *that*.

When he'd finished showering the Duchess with all the pretty things she deserved, as well as the kisses and other delights he had planned for her, she wasn't going to have a thought to spare for all that religious nonsense.

Brad stared grimly at the screen. Yes, the sooner he got her away from the green hill country, the better. All that religious stuff was crushing her down, holding her back. It might even give her some weird complex about *sex*, and that would be a tragedy.

He grinned suddenly. And he certainly intended to do everything in *his* power to make sure *that* didn't happen.

The sound of Delores knocking on his office door burst Brad's pleasant bubble. His lunch break, and his fantasies, were over. It was time to return to the real world.

But to his dismay, Brad found that returning to the real world was an increasingly difficult proposition. He thought of Jemima more than he liked to admit, more than was probably healthy for his ego, or his self-image as an independent bachelor.

That evening, back at his apartment, Brad pushed a TV dinner into his microwave and stared at it hopelessly. Even the "man sized" meat and potato meal was a sorry substitute for the food he remembered from the green hill country. He longed for Jemima's picnic basket with almost physical pain. And the memory of all the meals he'd had in Amish country haunted him – the ham and biscuits and pie and potato salad and chicken fried steak and...

Well, it brought tears to his eyes.

He flopped down at his kitchen table and put his chin on his fists. He thought the Amish were wrong about a lot of things, but food was one thing they got gloriously right.

He glowered at the humming microwave, and imagined the Duchess taking charge of his kitchen. It was a pretty fantasy.

If she did, no doubt the first thing she'd do would be to throw that microwave out as a tool of the devil, which it certainly was. Then she would insist on a brand new gas stove with all the bells and whistles, and would immediately turn his apartment into a home-cooking heaven.

Except that she wasn't *there*.

Brad chewed his lip. The Duchess had always messed with his mind, but to his dismay, her influence on his imagination was approaching critical mass. She was beginning to tint the way he saw the *world*. It used to be that he'd merely missed her when they were apart. But now, he was even beginning to see his apartment differently because of her.

It wasn't the biggest or nicest apartment in the world, that was for sure, but he'd been happy enough with it before he'd met the Duchess. Now, nothing about it seemed right without her.

Not even the microwave oven.

The microwave beeped and Brad rose and pulled the tray out of the oven. He peeled the plastic cover back gingerly.

His dinner stared back at him. It was a brown blob.

Brad leaned his head against the kitchen cabinet, and beat it against the door a time or two before he retired to the kitchen table for his evening meal.

CHAPTER ELEVEN

"Close your eyes now."

Brad smiled down at Jemima indulgently. She sat there with her brows raised, her eyes closed, and her lips slightly open – like a child.

She was *adorable*.

It was half past midnight, and they were huddled together in the office of her father's workshop, because it was snowing and bitter cold outside.

Her father's smithy was an extremely unromantic place – it was an unheated metal structure, and filled with large, heavy tools that looked to Brad like medieval instruments of torture.

But as far as he was concerned, *any* place with the Duchess was a desirable spot, and with blankets draped around them, and practically no space between them, the tiny side office had become very cozy indeed.

Brad reached down into the shiny gift bag he'd brought, and made tantalizing *crinkle* sounds to heighten Jemima's anticipation. "I bought this from a shop called *Angel Secrets*," he teased her, "because it reminded me of you, Duchess. Keep your eyes closed!"

Brad reached into the basket and pulled out a dainty box of gourmet chocolates. It had cost him almost 100 bucks, but each morsel was a work of art, and incredibly delicious.

His past experience with women had taught him, *when in doubt, overspend*. And, he figured that gourmet treats would warm Jemima up to the *other* gifts he planned to give her.

"Open your eyes!"

Jemima's eyes flew open, lighted on the beautiful chocolate box, and the bag brimming with treats, and looked up at him.

"Oh, Brad, they're beautiful!" she gasped. She picked the box up reverently. "Why, they're almost too beautiful to eat!"

"The key word being *almost*," Brad told her. He took the box, carefully removed the cellophane, and smiled at her. "Choose one."

Jemima scanned the box in delight. "I can't, they're all so pretty," she smiled.

"Then I'll choose one for you. *This* one," he murmured, picking out a small square of dark chocolate. Some *artiste* had placed a tiny candy raspberry on top – a delicate purple dot, surrounded by painted flowers.

"Open your mouth."

Jemima smiled and opened her mouth. Brad placed the confection square in the middle of that pink velvet, and Jemima's mouth closed around it.

Her eyes flew open. *"Ohhmm – dwishus!"*

Brad's smile faded. She really *was* just like a sweet, adorable – he shook his head, and the smile returned.

"Let's try this one next." He picked out a creamy white chocolate oval that had been painted with a forest scene, including a graceful deer.

"Here we go!" Jemima closed her eyes and opened her mouth again, and Brad placed the chocolate in her mouth.

"Ha!"

He caught himself up short, and shook his head. He was turning into a complete idi—

"Mmm, mmm," Jemima moaned, and opened her eyes. *"Cinnimum pecan crunch!"*

Brad smiled down at her indulgently. It was just as much fun to spoil Jemima as he'd imagined it would be, and he couldn't *wait* to give her more age-appropriate gifts.

But that was for later – when she'd gotten a little more *used* to delightful gifts.

"What's *this*?" he asked in mock surprise, pulling a bouquet of exquisite lollypops out of the bag. They were tiny, completely clear, and spangled with edible decorations like gold flakes, glitter, flowers, and herbs. They were painted as if they were book illustrations: with flying birds, and smiling cats, and children dancing, and a couple kissing. Jemima reached for them, and spread them out before her like a fan.

"Oh, Brad, where did you *get* these?" she cried. "I've never seen anything like them!"

Brad unwrapped the one with the kissing couple and passed it to her with a smile. "I was kind of hoping it would give you *ideas*," he told her, and Jemima laughed and kissed him, and then pressed her cheek to his.

"You're so *good*, and, and *generous*, Brad!" she murmured fervently.

Brad raised his brows wryly. He probably didn't deserve that kiss, but he was going to claim it anyway. He put his arms around Jemima, and kissed her back.

When they had finished exploring all the contents of the bag, and had traded kisses tasting of champagne marmalade, blackberry crème, and brown sugar pumpkin, Brad decided that it was time to put his broader plan into action. He smiled at Jemima and took her hands between his.

"Duchess, would you be willing to find out a *little* more about the Englisch world, if I was willing to find out more about your religion?"

The green eyes moved to him and held him.

"You want to learn about my religion?" Jemima asked in surprise. "I thought you were a – what was the word—"

"*Agnostic*, yes," Brad told her, smiling. "But I like to think I'm open-minded. I like to learn about what *other* people believe, too. Would you teach me?"

Jemima's eyes widened. "Oh *yes*, Brad," she breathed earnestly, "if you really want to learn."

"Oh, I do," Brad assured her, smiling. "But if I learn about your beliefs, will you listen to mine, too? Would you be willing to – say – learn more about the world?"

Jemima was beaming. "I guess that's only fair," she agreed, slipped a soft hand behind his neck, and kissed him so expressively that Brad forgot his plan. He put his arms around her, and pressed her to his chest, marveling how small and delicate she felt in his arms, and that his fingers *almost* met around her tiny waist.

"I'll give you all the books I can find," she was saying,

"*and* the newsletter, and if you have any questions, I'll do my best to answer them, even if I don't know them all. And if I don't know the answer, I can ask the bishop for you—"

Brad opened his eyes. "Ah ha, no, don't do that, Duchess!" he laughed. "I'm happy just to talk to *you*."

"Oh, yes, of course," Jemima laughed sheepishly. "It's just that I was so – you *really* want to know what we believe, Brad?"

"Yes, I really do, Duchess," he smiled. "We'll learn from each other. Does that sound fair?"

Jemima squeezed her eyes together in happiness. "Oh, *more* than fair!" she cried, and hugged him ecstatically.

Brad received her embrace and smiled up at the ceiling.

"I'm glad you agree," he told her. "I'll read your books, and you can come with me to a movie. Deal?"

She went still in his arms. "A movie?" she faltered. "But – we're not supposed to watch movies."

"Oh, well – I don't want to push you to do anything you aren't supposed to do," he conceded. "How about a trip to see a football game?"

He could feel her relax. "Oh, that would be wonderful," she agreed, in a relieved tone.

He turned his head and kissed her cheek.

"Perfect."

CHAPTER TWELVE

Jemima watched from the window of her father's workshop as the lights of Brad's truck faded down the road. Then she turned and gathered up all the evidence that they'd been there: the glittering bag, the lollypops, the jewelry-box of chocolate and the shiny wrappers.

She watched herself turn down the lantern, walk through the smithy and out into the snow. She saw herself turn and lock the door, walk between the big fir trees and across the yard to the house.

But it was all like a slow motion dream, like the big flakes of snow drifting down from the dark sky. She hardly even felt the cold.

Because Brad wanted to learn about being Amish.

She couldn't believe it!

For the first time, she felt a tiny spark of hope. If – by some miracle of God – Brad were to convert, then...

She closed her eyes. No, she couldn't let herself picture it. It would hurt too much to hope, and then have that hope dashed.

But Brad wanted to learn about being Amish.

She glided through the doorway and up the stairs like a sleepwalker. She entered her bedroom, dropped the quilts on the floor, and hid Brad's gifts away safe in the little nook behind the wall.

She came out of her cap and her dress and pulled on her nightgown. She crawled into bed and watched the big flakes of snow spiral past her window.

It was rare for an Englischer to convert, very rare, but it *had* happened. Oh, what if Brad decided to become Amish, and they got *married*, and they found a house of their own, and— She closed her eyes and smiled, and allowed herself to live in that happy fantasy until sleep took her, and Brad kissed her again in her dreams.

The next morning dawned bright and clear and cold. The sky was a clear, brilliant blue and the countryside was several inches deep in fresh, sparkling snow. By the time the sun was well up, the entire King household had made and eaten breakfast, and had been at work for well over an hour.

But Jacob King was distracted from his work by a troubling mystery. He came back to the house in an attempt to solve it.

"Has anyone been out to my workshop?" he asked.

Jemima had been wiping down the kitchen table, and she froze mid-swipe. She was no good at lying, and Deborah wasn't there to think of a quick excuse. She raised guilty eyes to her father's face.

Rachel shook her head. "I haven't been anywhere near it for the last two days," she replied. "Jemima, were you out there?"

Jemima dropped her eyes to the table. "I-I have no reason to go out there," she said softly. "Why do you ask, Daed?"

Jacob put one big hand to the back of his neck. "They've been snowed over pretty thick, but there are some kind of *prints* on the ground outside the shop. It looks like something was out there last night," he replied.

"Maybe it was an animal," Jemima ventured, but her heart was pounding.

"Maybe," Jacob replied. "But I don't like the idea of a stranger prowling around this house. Maybe it would be a good idea for us to get a watchdog."

Jemima felt her mouth falling open, and quickly closed it.

"Oh, it was probably a deer or a stray, Jacob," Rachel soothed. "Jemima's trouble is over now. Let it go."

Jemima made a desperate attempt to change the subject. "*Yes*, Daed, everything is back to normal now. The Englisch move so fast from one thing to another, they've forgotten all about me!

"When I give the rest of the money away, the last of it will be behind us. In fact, I was thinking – I was wondering – if you would drive me out to the bishop's house today?"

Rachel's eyes lit up. "Oh, what a *wonderful* idea!" she cried. "Did you hear that, Jacob? Jemima is ready to give away the last of the money, and to"—she turned to beam at her eldest daughter—"get back to her own life at last!"

Jacob shook his head. "I'm sorry, Mima. Not today. I have too much work piled up to drive you around the countryside. All this nonsense has put me back six months!"

Rachel's face fell, and she looked uncharacteristically put out. "Well then, if you're behind in your work, Jacob King," she asked him archly, "then why are you worried about a few marks in the snow? I would think you'd be in your shop, instead of here – teasing your poor daughter!"

Jacob looked wounded. "Now Rachel—"

"I'm not upset," Jemima interjected quickly, moving her eyes from her father to her mother. "I can wait, there's no hurry."

Rachel turned to her with her pretty mouth set. "Well, maybe there *should* be a little bit of a hurry, young lady," she retorted. "Those poor boys of yours are wondering when on earth you're going to give that money away. *I* wonder, too!

"And," she added, rounding on Jacob, "I would think that your *father*, of all people, would be willing to help you when it's something as important as your whole future – instead of hunting little snow goblins!"

Jacob crossed his arms. "I know what I saw, Rachel," he told her. "You can come and look at them, there are clear prints!"

To Jemima's astonishment, her mother began to giggle. "*Really,* Jacob," she replied softly, and giggled again.

Her father's face went as red as his hair, and he assumed an air of outraged dignity. He replied: "Laugh all you like, Rachel, but it's a good thing that I'm here to notice such things. There have been strange goings on around this house!"

Jemima lowered her eyes and held her breath, but that was her father's parting shot. He stalked out, and her mother stood silently drying dishes for a few long moments after.

Then she looked up at the ceiling, sighed, wiped her hands

on her apron and followed him outside.

Jemima crept to the window, silent as a mouse, to see if they would look at the telltale tracks she'd left in the snow. She put her ear to the window, and could make out the sound of soft talking. Then there was silence.

Jemima carefully pulled the curtains back, but to her astonishment, her parents weren't concerned with the prints in the snow at all. Her mother was in her father's huge arms, and any hurt feelings were clearly being mended.

Jemima smiled, and let the drapes fall closed, and returned to the kitchen table, but a deep sadness settled over her as she worked. Oh, *if only*, one day, she and Brad could kiss like that – on the porch of their own home!

CHAPTER THIRTEEN

For the next few days, Jemima withdrew from her family and friends in mind and spirit – even in body, when she got the opportunity. She slipped away to her father's study, or to her own bedroom, or to any quiet corner where she could be undisturbed.

Because she mostly didn't know what to do, and she was afraid to do what she *did* know.

She was praying like she'd never prayed before in her life.

Her father's study had always been her favorite retreat, especially on days when snowflakes drifted on the air.

Jemima slipped inside and closed the door behind her. The big red chair was invitingly empty, and a cozy fire crackled in the grate. She sank down into the softness of her father's huge chair, pulled her knees up under her chin, and watched the flames dance in the fireplace.

To Jemima's worried imagination, they seemed to form faces – faces that she knew and loved. She saw Joseph's handsome face break into a shy smile, Samuel's laughing eyes and quick grin, and Mark's quiet, steady gaze.

She closed her eyes and rested her head on her knees. *Oh please Lord*, she prayed, *Help me, I don't want to hurt any one of them. But I must. Show me how to do it the best way, the way that hurts them least!*

And Lord, give them new loves, all three, to heal their hearts. Give them all loving girls who'll adore them, and say yes right away when they propose.

Different girls from me.

She opened her eyes again. The flames crackled and leaped up suddenly, and she saw Brad's magnetic eyes in them, staring down at her. She gazed at them wistfully, but just as suddenly, they disappeared.

Oh Lord, I know I haven't done like I should. I've lied, and I've taken lots of money, and gone out with an Englisch boy who doesn't even believe in You, and all of that was wrong. Please don't be angry, and help me not to lie or do wrong again.

But I can't help seeing Brad, Lord. I love him so much it scares me sometimes, and that used to be wrong, Lord, but things have changed.

Now Brad says he wants to learn about being Amish, and he wants to learn about You. Oh, Lord, if you never hear another prayer of mine in all my life, please hear this one! Please, Lord – open Brad's heart!

Jemima opened her eyes. There was a faint sound from the doorway. The knob turned slightly, and then turned back. Soft voices filtered to her ears.

"No, don't go in, Jacob. Jemima's in there. I think she's praying, and we should let her. She has important decisions to make."

There was more soft murmuring, and the sound of retreating footsteps.

Jemima rested her head on her knees.

Lord, Brad had a terrible childhood, and his parents were very mixed up, and only You know what awful things that did to him. And he didn't have anybody to tell him about You, or to love him except his grandmother, and I don't know anything about her, but anyway, Brad says he's an ag— well, that word that starts with ag. You know!

Oh Lord, only You could ever know how much I want Brad

to become Amish, and to ask me to be his wife. But I would rather lose Brad and stay unmarried all my life, than to think of Brad going through his whole life without knowing how much You love him. Without knowing You at all! It breaks my heart to think of it, Lord, and I know it must break Yours.

Please, please, Lord, open Brad's heart!

And at dinner that evening, when they all bowed their heads to pray, Jemima's head remained bowed so long that Jacob finally had to clear his throat, and that had never happened before.

Jemima looked up quickly, colored faintly, and ate in chastened silence: but she noticed that her parents exchanged an awed look, and that Deborah's keen eyes were watching her narrowly.

She fixed her eyes on her plate and said nothing audibly. But she prayed:

Lord, please, please, open Brad's heart. Let us be married, so that one day I can look across my own table, and see the man I love smiling back at me!

That evening, in her own bedroom, Jemima unfurled her long hair and slowly plaited it, looking out over the snowy fields.

Oh Lord, I know I promised You that I'd give the money away, and I've been slow about that because I was sued, and I know that You know that wasn't my fault. But it's been almost a month since then, and now it is my fault, and I mean to fix that. I'll go to the bishop and give the rest of the money away, just like I promised.

In case You might be upset about that.

Though I don't really think You're worried about a month's delay.

But even so.

She wriggled into her nightgown, and pulled the covers back, and crawled inside, and turned down the lamp. She sighed, and stared up at the ceiling.

Lord, I will go to the bishop and give away the rest of the money. And while I'm there, I'll ask him if he would pray for Brad too, only I'll call him a friend, so the bishop won't know, and if you can't listen to my prayers because I messed up, then maybe You can listen to the bishop's prayers instead, because he's a good man and loves You very much.

Amen.

Jemima uncrossed her hands, and sighed and settled into her pillow.

CHAPTER FOURTEEN

The next day, Jemima rose early, about an hour before her usual time. She turned up the lamp in the freezing kitchen; built and lit a fire in her mother's cast iron stove, and the living room fireplace; and began to make breakfast. By the time her parents came downstairs, the kitchen was alight, cozy warm, and filled with the aroma of coffee and frying bacon.

"Well, well! What's this?" Jacob asked her, leaning over to plant a kiss on her cheek. "It looks like our Mima has come back to live with us."

Rachel opened up a cabinet and took out a frying pan. "Don't discourage her, Jacob. She'll be doing this in her own kitchen soon enough."

Jemima went pink, and smiled faintly, and poured out a cup of steaming coffee for her father. As she leaned over to give it to him, she asked lightly:

"Daed, I was wondering—"

He nodded. "Yes, *here* it comes!"

"—I was wondering, if today might be a better day for you to drive me to the bishop's house."

Jacob looked first at his daughter, and then at his wife, who was staring at him with a look that required no translation. He appeared to deliberate.

"Well – I might." He rubbed his chin with one hand. "I suppose I could find an hour or so to spare."

He was rewarded by his daughter casting herself on his chest with a display of surprising gratitude, and by another, much more pleasant look from his wife – the one that told him he was a *wise man*.

Bishop Lapp was one of the youngest men to ever rise to that position in the local district. He was a big, tall man, with a shock of bright blonde hair beginning to go gray at the temples, and bright blue eyes.

He was splitting wood in his front yard when their buggy

rolled up to his driveway. He paused, and wiped his brow with one arm, and leaned back on his axe handle to await them. His breath was like smoke in the chilly air.

Jemima peeped out of the buggy anxiously. She had seen Bishop Lapp before, but had never spoken to him, and had never been to his house. She looked him up and down, and felt a flicker of anxiety. He was as huge a man as her father. Maybe even a little taller. And he looked busy.

But a quick scan of the front of his house helped calm her flutters. A kind-looking brown-haired woman stepped out onto the porch behind them and waved. A little daughter of about five or six clung to her skirts.

Maybe Joseph Lapp wasn't *quite* as daunting he looked.

They climbed down out of the buggy, and Jacob held out his hand for her, and they walked together to greet the newly-minted bishop.

"Hello, Brother King," the bishop said pleasantly. He extended a hand, and her father shook it warmly. "It's good to see you and your daughter again. Would you like to come in, and have something hot to eat and drink?"

"Thank you, bishop," her father told him. "My daughter was very anxious to come and see you today. You've heard all the things that've happened to our daughter – how she got tangled up with the Englisch, and fell into so much money. Well, she says she wants to close the book on the whole thing, and give the rest of the money to the community fund."

The man's bright eyes moved to her face, and Jemima quickly dropped her own to the ground.

But the bishop's voice was kind. "That's a very generous offer," he said softly, and with a tinge of surprise. "Please, go on in, and make yourselves comfortable. I'll be there directly, and then we can talk."

He turned, and called to the woman on the porch. "Katie, we have company!"

The woman stood back and opened the door invitingly, and they hurried across the snowy yard and into the warmth of the big house.

A few minutes later they were warming their hands with cups of steaming hot chocolate and nibbling off plates filled with syrup-drizzled biscuits, cheese, and ham.

The bishop came in, wiped snow off his boots, and after he'd shrugged out of his coat and muffler, his wife gave him a cup of coffee and he folded himself up in a chair opposite the couch.

He took a long, appreciative sip, and trained those blue eyes on them. "Now, you say that Jemima here wants to give money to the fund. I can take care of that, if you're sure you want to do it, Jemima?"

Jemima raised scared eyes to his face. She nodded mutely.

"Well, then, you can come to my study and we can take care of it."

Jemima spoke up quickly. "Daed, I'd like to talk to the bishop privately – just for a minute," she told her father apologetically.

Jacob looked at her in surprise, but lowered himself back onto the couch. "Very well then, Mima," he told her.

The bishop stood up and extended a hand. "Come then."

Jemima followed the bishop into a large room with a big desk, a bigger chair, and lots of wall shelves, all crammed with books. The bishop pulled out a chair for her, and closed the door behind them.

He walked around to the desk, sat down in the chair and smiled a bit quizzically.

Jemima set her mouth. "I came to give you a check," she said, and reached into her purse. "It's all made out to the community fund – for whoever may need it to pay their emergency bills."

She extended the check in a small hand, and the bishop took it. He placed a pair of glasses over his nose, read the check, and lifted startled eyes to hers.

"This check is for—"

"I know how much it is," Jemima told him firmly. "I-I made a *promise to God*, and I'm here to fulfill it."

The bishop shook his head slightly, and then nodded. "Very well – if you're *sure*. I'll make out a receipt to show that the fund has received the money. I'll deposit it in the fund's bank account tomorrow morning. And I have to say," he added incredulously, "you've been *extremely* generous, young lady!"

He scribbled out a receipt, and handed it to Jemima over the desk. Then he looked a question, and Jemima went red.

"I-I also wanted to ask a favor of you," she said, in a small voice.

"Ask."

She lifted pleading eyes to his face. "First, will you promise me that this will be – just between *us*?"

He nodded. "All right. I won't tell anyone."

"I wanted to ask you to pray for a – a friend of mine," she urged. "This friend doesn't believe in God, but wants to learn more about Him, and – and about becoming Amish. Will you pray for them, bishop? Pray *hard*?"

The vivid blue eyes softened, and the bishop nodded. "Certainly, if you want. Would your friend, by any chance, be a young *man*?"

Jemima lowered her eyes, but could feel her face going bright red.

"I'm not asking you to tell me anything more," the bishop

said gently. "It's just that I once knew a young lady who *also* had a friend. Her friend didn't believe in God, either, and she hoped that he might come around, one day.

"But instead of her friend coming to God, it happened just the opposite. Her friend pulled her *away* from God, and away from her family. She got into more trouble than she could handle, and was very lucky to get away from him in the end."

Jemima kept her eyes glued to her hands, and said nothing.

The bishop sighed, and took off his glasses, and massaged his eyes with his fingers. "I'll pray for your friend, Jemima. But I'll also pray that God gives you the wisdom to put Him *first*."

"Thank you, bishop," she said, in a tiny voice.

He sighed again. "You're a very unselfish young lady, I can see that," he said, eyeing the check. "But sometimes you can be too unselfish for your own good. If your friend really *is* your friend, he won't ask you to do anything that's against what you believe.

"Remember that, Jemima."

"*I will, bishop*," she replied, in a voice almost too faint to be heard.

CHAPTER FIFTEEN

The lights of the stadium reached high up into the night sky, and far out to each side, with glaring white radiance. Brad pulled the truck into the last parking space left and turned off the motor.

He'd finally convinced Jemima to let him take her out on an *Englisch* date.

He reached back to get the ponchos he'd brought, because the night air was cold, but was struck by the Duchess' expression. She was leaning forward, peering up at the stadium in rapt wonder. He grinned and pulled the ponchos out.

"Pretty big, eh, Duchess?"

"I've never seen anything so big," Jemima breathed. "And the noise, it must be – well, I can hear it through the car door!"

"Yeah, it gets pretty crazy," Brad admitted, and handed her a poncho. "I brought these, because it's going to get cold. Ready?"

Jemima turned her big green eyes to Brad's face. He thought he saw excitement and just a little bit of *fear* in them. He reached out for her hand and gave it a squeeze.

"Come on."

Jemima smiled uncertainly.

Brad gave her a knitted cap to keep her ears warm, a silly little red thing with a long tassle, and thought she looked adorable in it. The big red poncho covered up that black getup she always wore, and for the moment at least, she looked just like anybody else.

Brad stared at her wistfully. If things went as he hoped they would, she'd soon be free to dress as she pleased, and to go anywhere she liked.

Because she'd be with *him*.

He pulled on his own knit cap and poncho, and took her hand.

He'd been careful to get good seats, pretty far down, and close to the 50 yard line. It was a college ball game, between his own school and their closest rivals, and it was getting close to kickoff.

He shouldered across the row of seated people, found their seats and helped Jemima get settled in. She was looking around at everything like a kid, and her eyes were as round as saucers. He smiled and leaned over.

"Do you know how football is played?" he asked.

She smiled and shook her head.

"Well, one team kicks the ball to the other team. And the team with the ball tries to move all the way down the field, to their goal line."

Jemima turned her big green eyes on him.

"Why?"

He felt his mouth slipping open. "Ah – well, to score points, and to win the game. The Miners and the Rockets are archrivals, so it should be a great contest."

"Which one do we want to win?" Jemima asked him, and Brad bowed his head and smiled.

"We're bigtime Rockets fans," he informed her gravely, and she nodded and picked up a plastic pompom.

"Rockets!" she cried.

Brad looked at her affectionately. He was hoping that this would be the first of many evenings out in the real world for Jemima.

He flagged down a vendor, and bought her a big cup of hot coffee and a hot dog, and the same for himself. He laughed at her reaction when the cheerleaders came prancing out on the field in their scanty outfits.

Her eyes got round, and her cheeks went pink and she was adorably embarrassed. To be fair, though, she was right – they had on very little, and it *was* cold. But for *his* money, not one of those glamour girls could compete with the Duchess, because their beauty depended on heavy makeup and a flashy wardrobe – things that seemed oddly garish, now that he'd grown used to her fresh-faced beauty.

The teams jogged out onto the field to the roar of the crowd, and everyone stood up and screamed. Brad laughed to see Jemima put her hands over her ears as the roar built like a wave to the point of kickoff – and then subsided.

Near the end of the first quarter there was a crushing tackle, and a man was down on the field. The medics and trainers rushed out onto the field, and Jemima stood up with one hand clapped to her mouth.

"Oh, Brad, something's wrong!" she cried. "They hit him too hard, he's *hurt*!"

Brad looked around them, smiling apologetically at the

people sitting behind them. "Yes, they're taking care of him, Duchess," he soothed, and slid a hand under her elbow. "You don't need to be upset."

Jemima allowed him to press her back into her seat, but insisted: "He's still down! Why do those boys play this game if it can hurt them?"

"He's all right – look, he's standing up now."

The player stood up slowly and was escorted off the field, to the applause of the crowd. Jemima seemed mollified, but when he glanced at her again, her head was bowed and her eyes were closed.

"What is it, Duchess?" he asked. "Are you feeling okay?"

She moved her lips, and then opened her eyes and looked up at him. "Yes, I'm all right."

"What were you doing?"

"I was praying for that boy who got hit," she replied earnestly. "And the others. I didn't know football was such a *dangerous* game!"

He couldn't help laughing, and leaned over and kissed her cheek, because he couldn't help that, either. "Of *course,*" he laughed.

After the game was over and the Rockets had won, and Jemima had enjoyed her first ever football game, and he'd been more entertained than he'd been in years, he'd had to drive her right back to her house. It was a long way back, and she had to get up at an insane hour.

But their farewell in the car had been warmer than ever, and more tantalizing. And before she had gone, he'd given her the little gold ring with the emerald chip. Her expression had been worth every penny of what it had cost him, and then some.

"*Oh, Brad,*" she'd gasped, and then rewarded him with another, very appreciative kiss. "Oh, I could never wear this, but I'll *always* treasure it. It's *so*—"

And she'd kissed him again.

That night, he lay awake on his bed, reliving it. He blew smoke rings toward the ceiling, and they magically transformed themselves into likenesses of Jemima. The way she'd looked in that silly red cap, the way she laughed at the dancing mascots and her mesmerized fascination with all the sights and sounds.

He could only hope that he was making headway, so that when it came time to ask her to leave home – to come away with him – he'd have a shot.

He turned on a little bedside light, sighed and picked up one of the many books the Duchess had given him as part of their deal. They were black and thick, and were crammed with hundreds of pages of tiny type and looked like they were a century old, at least.

There was also a copy of the local Amish newsletter. He leafed through it. It was filled with weather reports, crop news, recipes and livestock advice.

Yes, he was in love with the Duchess.

Nothing less than *love* could've made him crack such boring books, but he tilted up the cigarette, opened the first one and began to read.

CHAPTER SIXTEEN

The next weekend, Brad took Jemima out on another date to a county fair, and did all the things that a guy was supposed to do when he took his girl out to the fair: bought her cotton candy, won a stuffed animal to give her, and took her through the Tunnel of Love as often as she as willing to go.

Jemima screamed with laughter on the whirling teacups, had clung to him like a frightened kitten in the Fun House, and had gasped and whispered sweet things in his ear in the Tunnel of Love.

He'd given her the little vial of perfume, and she'd made all kinds of fuss over it, and then over him, and they had to move to a hidden spot, and had stayed there for a few delightful minutes.

A curling tendril of hair had escaped from under her cap, and he brushed it back, and asked her: "Having a good time, Duchess?"

She beamed at him. "Oh, Brad, the best time of my *life*!"

"We could do this sort of thing all the time, you know," he said casually – and waited. He didn't want to push his lady-love too much, or too soon. But to his dismay, she seemed not to take the hint.

Or what was more likely – she was being *polite*.

He smothered a sigh, and then smiled at her. "Ready for the House of Doom?"

"Oh, Brad," she whispered, and looked up at him with such serious dread that all his frustration vanished. He laughed, and kissed her, and promised: "Don't worry, I won't let anything *get* you."

And so he had saved her from the evil scarecrow and the clown with the maniacal laugh, and had smiled when she'd thrown her arms around him and buried her face in his shirt.

"Why do people even come to these *awful* haunted houses?" she'd wept, and he'd tightened his arms around her, and kissed away her tears, and forbore to point out the obvious.

The next week, he finally talked her into attending a movie

with him, but she had made him promise not to take her to something that involved people getting hurt, or stealing, or basically breaking any of the commandments. He had ended up taking her to a children's movie about a lost dog, and she had loved it.

After the movie, when he had driven to a pretty, moonlit spot and they were sitting together in his truck, he'd asked her to take her hair down again, and she had pulled out the pins that held it. That glorious, coppery hair had tumbled down like a waterfall, and he had taken it between his fingers, held it up to his mouth and inhaled its fragrance.

"I love your hair this way," he told her. "I wish you'd wear your hair like this *all* the time, Duchess. You *could*, you know," he added, and stared at her meaningfully.

Then he had presented her with the fluffy pink barrettes, and had begged to put them in her hair. She had blushed, and looked at her hands, and finally said *yes*; so he had slowly and reverently placed them in her silky hair.

They had been even prettier than he'd imagined, and he couldn't help wondering what Jemima would look like, if she dressed like any other woman. She'd be breathtaking – but a part of him was almost glad that she didn't.

He had *enough* competition already.

He raised his hand to caress her cheek, and she turned to him suddenly. She looked into his eyes so intently that he thrilled with the hope that she was going to throw herself into his arms. But instead, she knocked him completely off balance by asking the most unromantic and off-topic question he could imagine.

"Brad, did you—did you ever have time to – read the books and the magazine I loaned you?"

He raised his brows, sputtered a little and was glad that he'd taken the time, because he was able to say that he had.

She got shy suddenly, and looked down at her hands. "What did you *think* of them?" she asked.

He'd hesitated over his answer. He reminded himself that this was a *very* big deal for Jemima, and that it was important to be politic.

"Well, I think I got my head around the big picture," he told her cautiously. "I think I understand the main points of what you believe. And a lot of it is – is admirable. Really, I don't have a problem with most of it, because it's mainly the Golden Rule, and minding your own business, and working hard, and – all that kind of thing."

He stopped, and rubbed the back of his neck, and cast about in his mind for a way to change the subject. Religion always made him uncomfortable.

He looked over at Jemima, to see how his answer had gone down with her. She was still looking at her hands.

"I'm glad that you took the time to read them," she said at last, in a small voice. 'That was *very* sweet of you, Brad. I know you think – differently."

She looked at him just then, with something almost like hero worship in those big eyes, and he allowed himself to bask in the glow of her admiration – just a little.

He shrugged. "I try to keep an open mind," he told her nonchalantly. "It's part of my training as a reporter."

The part of his brain that policed idiocy struck him smartly upside the head. He caught himself and winced, imagining what Delores would've made him suffer, if she'd caught him preening about his "training as a reporter."

But of course, Jemima knew no different. She beamed at him.

"Oh, Brad, it really is so good of you to – to see our side," she told him warmly, taking his hand. "Most people on the outside don't even try," she added sadly. "They just laugh, and make fun of us, or, or seem to be *fascinated*, which is almost as bad. They ride by our house sometimes on tour buses and point at us, as if we're some kind of exhibit in a museum."

Her eyes looked unbearably forlorn, and he leaned over and kissed the sad look away and stroked the softness of her hair.

"Not cool," he told her sympathetically. "*So* not cool."

"I really appreciate that you try, Brad," she sighed, pillowing on his chest. "That at least you take the time to *try* to understand why we're different. It means a lot to me."

"Anything to oblige," he murmured, and caressed a silky skein of that amazing hair.

"I *mean* it," she answered, and turned to look at him. She held his face in her hands and looked into his eyes. Her expression was serious.

"I pray for you *every* day, Brad," she whispered. "I pray a *long* time. I pray that one day, you really will understand. That you'll know God for *yourself*."

He sighed, and looked down at her. It was adorably sweet, and it melted his heart; and it simultaneously made him intensely uncomfortable. So he'd stopped Jemima's mouth with a kiss.

That sweet, silky mouth had made all the words slide away, made them the only two people in the world, made his hands itch to wander, but he forced himself to exercise restraint. *That* part had always been hard, and now it was approaching torture, but something else, something stronger, held him back.

Love, yes – but more than love. The dawning suspicion that the delight of discovery was keenest, most intense, when it was achingly *gradual*.

He was falling in love with Jemima by delicious inches, a

little more every time they were together. He felt privileged to witness her delight as she turned her face to the world for the first time – like a flower opening up to the sunlight. She was blooming into womanhood before his eyes, like a young rose.

Brad looked down at her as their lips parted. She beamed up at him, laughing, her beautiful eyes alight.

He wanted to be the one to carry her through that last door. It would be a supremely tender moment, and even in imagination, it was precious to him. He'd planned it a hundred times, but had always turned away.

Because he was coming more and more to the conclusion that he wanted to marry Jemima. And for once in his life, he wanted to be unselfish.

He wanted to give Jemima what *she* had imagined.

CHAPTER SEVENTEEN

That evening Brad lay on his bed, shirtless, wearing a rumpled pair of plaid pajama bottoms. It was almost 2 a.m., but he was wide awake – smoking and assessing his plans for the future.

He shook his head. A year ago, if anyone had told him that he'd *long* to get married, he would've laughed. He was probably the world's unlikeliest candidate for matrimony.

He'd never felt the smallest temptation to follow his parents' example. Their marriage had been a case study in dysfunction. His memories of his father were few and dim – a pair of unhappy blue eyes, looking down at him, hands that held him carelessly and echoes of shouted obscenities and slamming doors.

His father had been a loud, unpleasant haunting in their home. And then one day, just like *that*, he'd disappeared like a ghost, leaving Brad and his mother to live in an ever-widening pool of silence.

Brad blew a contemplative smoke ring toward the ceiling, thinking that it really was kind of a miracle that he didn't have a complex toward women, after all his Mom had put him through. Her meth addiction had turned him into a seven-year-old adult who knew way too much about booze and drugs and whose biggest talent wasn't baseball or soccer, like other kids, but a knack for hustling money from people who didn't pay attention.

His mom had spent most of his childhood in a drugged stupor, and when the state had finally stepped in and taken him away from her, he'd felt nothing but sorry for her – and relieved for himself.

A few months later, she was dead.

He'd lived with his grandmother for awhile, and he'd been fond of her. She had been a stern, strong old woman with a booming voice and no patience for nonsense. But she'd provided him a stable home, and as much affection as it was in her nature to show.

She'd encouraged him to find a trade, to start work, to make something of himself and to stop trying to take advantage of other people. He smiled to himself. That teaching had only *half* taken. He'd been doing it for so long that he didn't know how to stop.

But when he'd had a chance to get a scholarship from a local school, his grandmother had encouraged him to apply. And when he'd won, she had put up some of her own money to send him. Yeah, she'd kind of saved him.

She was dead now, too, and he missed her.

He inhaled deeply, and the embers of the cigarette glowed.

Now, he'd met the Duchess, and maybe had a chance to build something like a family with her. If he could convince her to marry him, and to live with him.

Jemima couldn't possibly be the angel that she *seemed* to be. He wasn't *that* far gone. But she was still the most unselfish, sweet-tempered person he'd ever met. Her beauty made those qualities even rarer, and more to be admired.

It was kind of like that verse he'd read out of the hotel room Bible, the one about the good woman who was worth more than rubies. The writer might've been talking about Jemima. She really was a rare jewel.

If only she wasn't so *religious*. That, *that* was the only thing that still stood between them, and it was the one thing that might still ruin his chances.

Their last few months together had been nothing short of

amazing, and he was tempted to call them a success. Jemima had told him that she loved him. She gave the impression that she was walking in a dream when they were together. She'd expressed nothing but delight when she was with him, and had been appreciative of even his smallest effort to please her.

When he took her out to experience a world she didn't know, she didn't seem to suffer culture shock. She'd never objected to any place he'd taken her. She had a childlike openness to new experiences, as long as they weren't forbidden by her church.

He frowned, sputtered smoke, and tamped out his spent cigarette.

But in spite of all of that, he had the sense that his relationship with Jemima had reached an impasse. He reached over to the nightstand and pulled out a fresh cigarette.

After weeks of retail romance, he had to conclude that flowers and candy and gifts hadn't been enough to move her.

Jemima was humoring him, he could *feel* it. She never expressed any curiosity about the Englisch world. She never asked questions about it, she never begged him to show her more of it, and she still wore her traditional dress, even when they went out together.

In spite of all his efforts to win her over to the world, Jemima hadn't shown the slightest sign that she'd be willing to abandon her beliefs, or leave her home for him.

In short – he was *in trouble*.

He sighed. Every time he'd tried to gently suggest a different life for her, she'd looked at him with that blank, polite expression that promptly ended the discussion. He didn't get the sense that she was trying to be coy – she was the most genuine person he'd ever met.

Maybe the trouble was that he'd been too general, too vague. Maybe she didn't yet understand *exactly* what he'd been trying to say.

He chewed his lip. If he asked her to *elope* with him, to leave her home, there'd be no doubt in her mind what he was asking. Her choices would be clear.

It was a long shot, he knew that, but he told himself that it wasn't *impossible*, that some people *did* leave the Amish church. There were whole *TV shows* built around them.

But on the other hand – it would be risky. If Jemima said *no*, there would be no alternative, nothing left for him to suggest. There was no way that he could be part of her world.

It would be *over* between them.

And that was why he was chain smoking in his bed at 2 a.m.

Brad sighed, crushed out his cigarette, and turned off the bedside light. Then he folded his arms behind his head and stared up at the dark ceiling for awhile.

On an impulse, he prayed: *God, if you exist, I could use a little help here.*

Then he laughed at himself, shook his head, and closed his eyes.

CHAPTER EIGHTEEN

Jemima slipped into the house through the back door and closed it softly behind her. She had just returned from a date with Brad. It was after midnight, and her shoes were dangling from her hands as she tiptoed up the stairs and down the long moonlit hall to her own bedroom door.

She slipped safely inside and placed her shoes carefully under the bed. Then she trimmed the lamp, and lit it, preparing to undress.

But to her surprise, she wasn't the only one up late. There was a soft tap at the door. Jemima's heart quickened in alarm, and she padded to the door and pressed her face to the crack.

"Who is it?" she whispered.

"It's *me*, stupid."

Jemima opened the door, Deborah stood there in her nightgown. She pushed in as soon as the door was open.

Jemima closed the door behind her, and looked at her sister with some irritation. "What is it? Why are you up at this hour?"

Deborah gave her a shrewd look. "I could ask *you* the same question! You've sure been sneaking out a lot lately. I'm surprised how much you're pushing your luck."

"It's late, Deborah," Jemima told her. "What do you *want*?"

"You're skating on such thin ice that I just want to review some facts before I skate out on the ice with you. You've decided on the *Englisch* boy, that's your final decision? You're *sure* you're not sneaking out with Samuel or Joseph or Mark?"

Jemima pinched her lips into a thin line. It was a crazy hour of the night to have this conversation, it was none of Deborah's business *who* she loved, and she had no idea why Deborah was interested *anyway*.

But she didn't dare tell her so. Deborah had too much *on* her now to be challenged. She took a deep breath, and nodded. "I've decided. It's *Brad*."

Deborah looked oddly relieved. "Well, what are you going to do with the others? It won't take long for word to get out that you've given away all your money. All three of those guys are going to be coming here to court you again. You're not going to be able to put them off for long."

Jemima bit her lip. Deborah was right, but for the wrong reason. She should've told her friends the truth as soon as she knew it herself. It was cruel to keep them in suspense.

"I'm not going to try to put them off," she answered. "I'm going to tell them all. It isn't fair to them to delay."

"I agree," Deborah mused. "Go ahead and tell them – the sooner the better! But it's going to be harder to meet your Englisch boy on the sly once you've cut them all loose," she added. "You have to be prepared for that. Mamm is holding Daed off because she thinks you're meeting *Mark* or *Samuel* every weekend. She's *covering* for you – or haven't you noticed?"

Jemima gasped and looked at her sister in dismay. Deborah shook her head.

"You really *are* in your own little world, aren't you?" she marveled. "But you better wake up quick, if you don't want things to blow up on you. You have to be extra careful. If Daed catches you with that Englisch boy, *then* there'll be fireworks!"

Jemima shuddered. "Don't even *say* it!" she murmured

fervently.

Deborah bit one thumbnail. "Daed might kill him," shrugged. "I'd give it fifty-fifty odds."

Jemima sat down on the bed, and brushed her hair a little harder than necessary. "You all talk like Brad is some, some kind of *housebreaker*. He's a *fine* man. He says he wants to learn about becoming *Amish*," she said.

Deborah glanced at her, but said nothing.

"He really *is* interested!" Jemima added defiantly.

"So *you're* not going to be the one to change?" Deborah frowned. "I thought you were going to, I don't know, run away with him and get married and live with the Englisch. Do you really think he could live like us?"

Jemima stopped brushing and stared into space. She really didn't know the answer to *that* question.

"If I were you, which God forbid," Deborah said devoutly, "I'd be thinking about how I was going to meet Brad after you set all those other boys free, because Mamm will be so mad at you for throwing them away that not *only* will she stop holding Daed back, she'll be watching you *herself*."

Jemima's eyes widened. She hadn't thought of *that*.

"Oh, *Debby*," she gasped.

"*Mmm-hmm*. So, you need to be setting things up *now*,

before you let the others go, so Mamm can okay your outings before she knows what they're really *for*."

Jemima hung her head sadly. "Oh, Deborah, you make it sound so – so *sneaky*."

"Do you want to see him, or not?"

"Oh, I *have* to see him!"

Deborah sighed and looked at her ruefully. "You are my sister, Jemima, but *honestly*. God knew what he was doing when he made you beautiful," she mused, "because you are the woolly lamb of the *world*. You're lucky I'm here to hold your hand, or things would've gone bad for you long before now."

Jemima looked up at that, and eyed her sister doubtfully. "Why *are* you helping me?" she asked. "You never gave me an explanation that made any sense. Why do you care if Brad and I get together?"

Deborah gave her a shrewd look, as if she was weighing her answer. After a long moment, she shrugged.

"Because I'm in love with *Mark*, that's why!"

"*What?*"

"If you'd been paying any attention at all, you would've seen it," Deborah told her, shaking her head.

"Oh, Debby, I didn't dream—" Jemima wailed softly.

"Why didn't you *tell* me?"

Deborah gave her such a wry look that Jemima felt her own face going hot. "*Oh – yes.* I guess it would have been – very awkward."

"I know it's a hopeless case," Deborah sighed forlornly, flopping down on the bed, "but I figured that if you didn't want him *yourself,* maybe you could put in a good word for me – here and there."

Jemima pursed her lips and nodded. *Now* the mystery was solved. *That* explained everything. But, even if Deborah *was* a scheming little imp, and bad-tempered and rude and not above lying, and lazy and manipulative and generally not to be trusted – she still *was* her sister.

Though to tell the truth, she didn't know if there was much good she could honestly tell Mark about Deborah. But – then again – maybe Debby had been all those wrong-headed things because she'd been in love with Mark, and had to watch him fall in love with someone *else.* It must have been *very* trying.

She decided to give Deborah the benefit of the doubt.

"Well, Debby," she said softly, "here's what I can do, and I think it will work out the best. I'll tell you what kind of girl Mark likes, and maybe you can – try to be more like *that.*

"Mark is very conservative. He likes a girl who has a *sweet, pleasant personality,* who says *nice* things about other people, who doesn't *complain.*"

Deborah gave her a dry look, but said nothing.

"He likes to be the one to lead. He likes modesty, and a girl who holds to traditional ways." She gave Deborah a meaningful look.

"And most of all – *Mark hates lying*, and can smell it a *mile* off!"

"*Hmmm*," Deborah said primly. "I guess we're *both* in trouble, then."

CHAPTER NINETEEN

Jemima sat sewing on the couch in the living room. The sound of a horse's hooves on the road outside made Rachel walk to the front door and peek out the glass pane, but Jemima continued to sew.

"Why, it looks like Joseph Beiler," she murmured. Then she pursed her lips, and turned to her daughter.

"But that wasn't news to you, was it, Mima?" she asked, and then nodded knowingly. "Yes, I can see that it wasn't. I'll make sure that no one interrupts the two of you," she smiled.

Jemima didn't look up. "Thank you, Mamm," she murmured.

But after her mother was gone, Jemima sighed deeply. She'd decided to take Deborah's advice and break it off with her admirers, at last.

She'd written Joseph a short note a few days ago, asking him to come to the house. She dreaded this meeting, and hated to hurt Joseph – sweet, *smitten* Joseph – but she couldn't let him go on thinking that she was going to marry him.

She heard him park the buggy into the yard, and after a few minutes, the sound of his footsteps crunched over the snow. She almost smiled. Joseph had such *big* feet.

The porch steps creaked under him, and his knock at the door sounded loud in the stillness. Jemima put away her sewing, and rose to answer it.

Joseph was standing in the doorway, his dark eyes shining. His cheeks were rosy with the cold, and Jemima stared at him wistfully. He really was *so* handsome.

She tried to smile. "Come in, Joseph," she murmured, and held the door open.

Joseph took off his hat, and scraped the snow off his boots politely, and stepped in.

"Come and sit with me," she invited, and motioned toward the couch.

He sat down quickly, and she sat down beside him. He

searched her face with his eyes, and his smile faltered.

"What's this I see?" he said quietly, and took her chin gently in his hand. "You look – *sad*."

Jemima turned her head, and his hand fell away. "I *am* sad, Joseph," she answered softly. "I have to tell you something that will hurt you, and I hate to do it. We've been such good friends, and I wouldn't hurt you for the world."

His eyes registered confusion. "What could make my *maus* sad?" he asked, and reached for her hand, but she wouldn't let him take it.

Jemima closed her eyes. She couldn't bear to see his reaction.

"I asked you here to tell you – that I can't marry you, Joseph," she said simply. "I can't let you make plans, and buy a house, and – and go on thinking that we're engaged."

There was no sound at all. Jemima took a deep breath, and when she opened her eyes, Joseph was looking down at his hands. Her heart ached for him.

He shook his head, once. "How can that be?" he asked brokenly. "How? After all that's passed between us?"

"Joseph, I-I've always been so *fond* of you, but – I've searched my own heart, and I'm not in love with you, at least, not enough to be your wife. I can't marry you. It wouldn't be fair," she whispered.

"But – but why *not*?" he asked.

If it had been a less painful conversation, she might almost have sputtered out a fond laugh. Joseph was so sweet and naïve – like a child, sometimes.

When she didn't answer, he looked up, and there was a tinge of anger in his eyes. "There's someone else, isn't there, Mima?" she asked.

Tears blurred her eyes, and she looked away. He nodded.

"You don't have to tell me – I can *see* it," he growled. "Who is it, Mima? *Who* stole you away from me?"

"Joseph, please—"

"No, Mima, I have to know. Because I'm not going to give up so easy. I'm going to fight to keep what's mine!"

"Joseph—"

He stood up suddenly, looked up at the ceiling, then down at her. "If you won't tell me, I'll find out myself. No matter what I have to do, this isn't over. Somehow, I'll make you change your mind, Mima."

Jemima put her hands over her face and shook her head. "Oh, Joseph, *don't*," she cried, but he had already stalked out. The sounds of his receding footsteps were followed by the crack of a buggy whip, and the sound of his horse's hooves clattering over the snow.

Jemima turned into the sofa cushions and cried brokenheartedly. After awhile her mother came in softly, took one look, and sat down beside her on the couch. Jemima went wordlessly into her arms.

"So it wasn't Joseph," her mother soothed, rocking her back and forth. "My poor girl. Telling a friend you're *not* going to marry him is one of the hardest things a woman must do."

She turned her head and kissed her daughter. "But I know that you did it as kindly as you could, my Mima," she soothed.

"Oh, Mamm," Jemima sobbed, "you should have heard him! He wouldn't accept what I told him! He says he's not giving up so easy, and he's going to *fight*!"

"He'll come to accept it, Mima," her mother answered calmly. "He will, eventually. Right now he's hurt and confused. But when he's had time, he'll be all right. You'll see."

"I feel so awful," Jemima sobbed, "like I've *murdered* him somehow. I don't know how I'm going to do this—"

Jemima gasped, and caught herself just in time. She had been on the brink of saying, *I don't know how I'm going to do this – two more times.*

"You've been so sought after, Mima," her mother sighed. "And this is the hard part. But once it's over, the easy part comes. The joyous time comes, when you can say *yes* to the boy you love."

Jemima stared over her mother's shoulder, wide-eyed. "Will it?" she whispered.

"*Of course*, dear," her mother soothed.

CHAPTER TWENTY

Jemima gave herself a few days to recover from her painful parting from Joseph. She spent her days in quiet, repetitive work that required no mental concentration. She washed and ironed, she mopped and dusted, and she helped her mother make dough for baking.

She shunned society, and whenever she was able, she stole away to her own bedroom, or her father's study. She had never felt in such urgent need of prayer; but she also felt a growing sense of guilt over her delay.

She planned to tell Samuel next. But telling *him* was going to be even harder than telling *Joseph*.

Because she loved Samuel, had loved him since they were children. It was impossible *not* to love the mischievous blond boy with the twinkling blue eyes and ready charm. He'd been a fixture at their house for years – swinging his legs over their porch rail, sitting at their table, snitching cake from the fridge.

Filling the house with the sound of his jokes and laughter.

It was going to be *lonely* when he wasn't there anymore. But Jemima told herself that such thoughts were selfish. So she gathered her strength and mailed Samuel a note.

He arrived on the afternoon of the next day. It was a greeting-card November afternoon, with big flakes of snow falling from a leaden sky.

She had chosen to talk to him in her father's cozy study, where they could be alone. She'd prepared cups of hot coffee and built a crackling fire, in the forlorn hope that the *warmth* at least would be of some comfort to him.

She sat in the study, listening to the sounds of his progress to the house and then the jaunty rapping that was his familiar knock at the door. The sound of her mother's greeting, and his own respectful reply.

The sound of his footsteps across the floorboards of the living room. Samuel had a quick, light step.

The sound of a second rapping – softer this time – on the study door.

She lifted her head. "Come in, Samuel."

The door opened and Samuel filled the space inside it. He was holding his hat, and his mop of blond hair caught the firelight and glistened like gold. Jemima looked up at him wistfully, forced herself to smile, and motioned toward her father's chair.

"Please sit down, Samuel. I have coffee, if you're cold."

Samuel accepted the cup gratefully, warmed his hands on it and took an appreciative sip. "Thanks Mima," he grinned. "It's cold outside. Coffee just hits the spot."

She let him warm himself. She listened wistfully as he told a funny story about a fox that burst out of the bushes and spooked his horse on the way over, and how he'd almost set a world record, until he could get it under control. She smiled sadly, watching him, thinking: *It's the last time.*

When he'd finished his story she smiled, and bowed her head, and prayed: *Lord, help me do this. I don't know if I can.*

Samuel laughed again, and took another sip of coffee. "So why did you ask me over, Mima? A note, too! It sounded *official.*"

He turned to look at her, and the smile gradually faded from his eyes.

Jemima prayed again, and looked up into his eyes.

"I wanted to talk to you alone, Samuel," she murmured. "I

need to let you know – that I've made a decision." Her eyes filled with tears.

"I'm *sorry*, Samuel," she went on, "but I can't marry you. I'm in love with another man."

Samuel's beautiful blue eyes widened. Jemima watched as a dozen emotions chased each other across their swirling surface – hurt, disbelief, shock, and – loss. Samuel bowed his blond head, and his hands hung limply over the edge of the armrests.

"Samuel, I'm *so*—"

His sandy brows rushed together. "Who is it, Mima?" he asked huskily. "Not Joseph, surely. So it must be Mark."

Jemima dropped her gaze to her lap and said nothing, but to her relief, Samuel didn't press her.

"I hope the two of you are – very happy together. I mean that, Mima." He turned to her, leaned over, and kissed her cheek.

Jemima put a hand to his face as he kissed her. "Oh, Samuel, I hope that when – when some *time* has passed, we can go back to being friends," she whispered, turning pleading eyes to his face. "I've always been *so* fond of you."

He looked down, shook his head, and smiled crookedly. "It might not be right away, Mima," he said softly.

"Just so long as we *can* still be friends," she replied. "But I can't see it being very long, Samuel," she murmured fondly. "You're too sweet and handsome to be without a girl for long."

He looked at her and smiled gallantly. "You're probably right, Mima," he rallied, and in spite of her tears, Jemima laughed a little.

"I know I'm right. Miriam Zook has had her eye on you for years," she told him, "and I'll probably still be jealous if I see the two of you together. But I'll just have to live with it."

Samuel looked up at her. "Mark is a lucky man," he told her ruefully. "I hope he understands that."

Jemima looked down and made no reply.

Samuel nodded. "I hope you won't think I'm rude if I leave a little early," he told her. "I think I need to go home and lick my wounds for awhile." He turned, looked at her affectionately, and caressed her cheek with his hand.

"Best of luck, Mima."

"And you, Samuel," Jemima told him, with tears in her eyes.

She watched him as he walked out of the room, so tall and straight and handsome, and was stabbed by a sense of terrible loss. There had been no other way – but *even so*.

The tiny crackle of the fireplace suddenly sounded loud in his absence.

Jemima listened for Samuel's voice as he said his farewells to her parents in the living room. She heard the screen door creak open and slap shut. She heard Samuel's slow footsteps fade gradually across the yard.

The thought that she would never hear them coming back, was almost too sad for her to bear.

Dinner that evening was subdued and mostly silent. Jemima was oppressed with a heavy sense of sadness and said almost nothing, and Deborah spoke only on command, but Jacob and Rachel exchanged knowing glances. Rachel maintained a silence that was respectful of Jemima's melancholy mood, but it was clear that she was *glowing* with suppressed excitement.

Deborah's wary eyes flitted occasionally to her mother's face, and then to her father's, and then to Jemima's – but she said nothing.

CHAPTER TWENTY-ONE

The next morning after breakfast, Rachel bustled around the house, humming happily. Occasionally her voice welled up into song.

"Sister dear, never fear, for the Savior is near,
With His hand He will lead you along;
And the way that is dark Christ will graciously clear,
And your mourning shall turn to a song."

Jemima looked up from her mending and met her mother's happy eyes. Rachel dimpled at her, and turned back to her work.

"For that home is so bright, and is almost in sight,

And I trust in my heart you'll go there."

Jemima lowered her eyes submissively, but couldn't endure her mother's cheerfulness for long. She excused herself, pleading a headache, and went upstairs to her bedroom where she could think in peace.

She closed her bedroom door behind her and walked to the window overlooking the countryside. The porch roof, the yard and the hills beyond were covered with snow, and in the predawn light, they had taken on a pale blue cast. Here and there, in the folds of the hills, smoke rose faintly from their neighbors' chimneys.

It was nearing Thanksgiving, and Jemima knew that she had *many* things to be thankful for. But it was hard to remember them, because the dread of her final duty weighed on her like a lead weight.

She had to tell Mark that she couldn't marry him, and it would be the hardest thing she'd ever done in her life. Of all her suitors, she was the closest to Mark. She and Mark understood one another so well that sometimes they didn't even need to say anything.

Some people expected them to get married because of that. Some people had *already* assumed that they were engaged.

And that was why she had to talk to Mark, whether she felt like it, or not. Otherwise, her mother might let slip what she was clearly thinking, and *that* would be terrible.

Jemima leaned her brow against the freezing window pane, praying for guidance; but the sky didn't open, and no clear instructions formed in her mind.

But when she opened her eyes, a small, dark figure below made her stand up straight. It was a man in dark coat and hat, walking across the yard to the porch.

Jemima's heart sank. *It was Mark.*

She closed her eyes. She didn't need to ask why he'd come, she knew it in her bones. He'd come to get his answer, and it was just like him to take the initiative. He never could endure waiting.

The living room was directly below her, and she could hear and *feel* Mark climbing the porch steps, stomping the snow off of his boots, and knocking at the door.

Jemima brushed her hand across her eyes, and smoothed back her hair. She had to get Mark out of the house, or her parents would know at once that they weren't engaged, and weren't *going* to be, and she wasn't ready for that scene. It would also spare Mark the necessity of having to make small talk with her family.

She quickly put on her heavy cape, then turned and went swiftly downstairs.

"Well, good morning Mark!" Rachel was saying.

"Good morning," Mark replied. His eyes met Jemima's

over Rachel's shoulder as she came quickly down the stairs.

"Good morning, Mark," Jemima said, as cheerfully as she could. She turned her face to her mother's. "Mark promised to take me on a buggy ride this morning through the snow," she smiled.

Mark's expression revealed no hint of surprise, and Jemima blessed him silently.

"Why, that sounds lovely," Rachel smiled, and kissed her daughter's cheek. "Try to be back by lunch!"

"We will," Jemima said over her shoulder. She took Mark's arm, and shuttled him out of the front door almost as fast as he'd come in.

They walked down the porch steps, and across the yard, and Mark helped her up into the buggy before asking: "What was that all about?"

Jemima couldn't meet his eyes. "I wanted to talk to you alone," she replied softly. "I wanted to get out of the house."

Mark climbed up into the buggy and turned to her. "Where do you want to go?"

"It doesn't have to be far," Jemima answered, and he shook the reins.

They turned right off the lane, and the buggy rolled over the snow better than any car could have. Soon the high banks blocked the King farmhouse from sight, and the last window faded from view.

Mark pulled the buggy around the big curve, and past the fallow field where, unbeknownst to him, Brad had cut many a path coming to see her. They rounded the curve, and to Jemima's chagrin, Mark parked the buggy in the very spot where Brad always parked his truck.

He pulled the horse to a stop, looped the reins over the dash. He sat without saying anything for a few long moments. Finally he turned to her, with those sapphire eyes that saw so clearly. Jemima felt her throat tightening, because the truth was in those eyes.

Mark knew.

"I just thought I'd come over. I got tired of waiting, Mima," he said at last. "Better to just get it over with."

She couldn't meet his eyes. "*I'm sorry,* Mark," she whispered.

He was still looking at her steadily. "It's the Englisch guy, isn't it, Mima," he asked, "the reporter?"

She still couldn't meet his eyes, and couldn't deny it. He nodded.

"I had a feeling," he said slowly. "I could tell by the way you were acting. You never acted that way with me, and I never saw you act that way with anybody else. And when I saw you *looking* at him in the courtroom that day, I knew you'd decided. When you wouldn't talk to any of us after, I was sure."

Jemima shook her head. "I'm sorry, Mark," she whispered. "I should've told you sooner, I should've let you know. It's just that – I didn't know myself at first. It happened so fast, and I still don't know how it will end. It makes no sense to love an Englisch boy, but I can't help it. I *can't*. I'm sorry."

He looked at her, and his expression didn't convey whether he was feeling sad or angry or merely empty.

He reached out and took her hand. "I won't lie, Mima. It hurts. But I don't blame you, and I'm not mad. You have a right to fall in love with any guy you like. Even if he's – not me."

Jemima looked up at him through red eyes. "Don't hate me, Mark. I never meant to hurt you!"

He looked faintly surprised. "Hate you, Mima? No, that's impossible. I've already tried, and I can't do it."

"Oh, *Mark*!" she sobbed, and he lifted a gloved hand, and brushed the tears off her cheek.

"A girl as beautiful as you should never have to cry," he told her softly. "And if it doesn't work out between you and that guy, Mima, you know where I am," he told her.

He raised his dark brows and smiled.

"One last time," he murmured, and before she could react,

Mark's lips were warm on hers – as always, communicating with actions what he could not say in words.

CHAPTER TWENTY-TWO

Brad picked up his jacket and shrugged into it. It was freezing outside, and he'd forgotten to bring his lunch, so it was time to make the punishing trek from the front doors of the *Ledger*, to the warm, steamy interior of Mama Wong's Chopstix Heaven, two blocks down on Main.

He shouldered through the revolving door in the lobby and was hit immediately with an icy blast. He dug his hands into his pockets and put his head down against the wind.

He got about halfway there, and had to wait at a street crossing for the light to change. There was a jewelry store on the corner, just a little hole in the wall, really, but the display in the window caught his eye.

There was a delicate diamond ring glittering under a spotlight. It was tiny, elfin, and as it turned back and forth on a revolving stand, it threw off sparks of pure white light.

Brad stared at it, and kept staring, even after the light changed. But when the people waiting beside him started to move, he followed quickly. It was too cold to window shop.

Brad crossed the windy street, dove into the restaurant on the other side, and was glad when the heavy doors of Mama Wong's closed behind him. Warmth and noise reached out and enveloped him. He followed the waitress to a booth in the back, pulled out his smart phone, and settled in.

The waitress soon reappeared with warm coffee and a menu, and he ordered a big bowl of noodle soup and a platter of Mongolian beef. The girl took his menu and disappeared.

Brad checked his messages, searching for a call from a Lancaster County prefix, but there was none. He sighed and scrolled back up to the top.

Junk, junk, spam. More spam, junk, one laughable email from an English "estate lawyer," a threatening message from Delores.

He backed up and read that one.

Brad, I don't know why you're evil with Eddie, but if you send him out to take photos of a sewage treatment plant, you'd better have a good reason next time, or it's coming out of your paycheck.

He grinned and scrolled down further. More spam, a magazine article he'd never read, and – an email from Sheila. His brows went up. He hadn't expected to hear from *her* again.

The waitress returned with the soup and the platter. She set them on the table in front of him. They looked delicious, and they were fragrant of soy sauce, shallots and braised beef. Brad turned off the phone and turned his attention to his lunch.

A few minutes later, after he'd taken the edge off his hunger, his mind began to wander again. To Jemima, as it inevitably did, when there wasn't some other urgent interruption.

He wondered what she was doing at that moment, and wished for the thousandth time that he could call her, but she'd refused to accept a cell phone, refused even to use one. Some silliness about being *connected to the world*. Which, apparently, was a mortal sin.

He frowned. The cell phone was a small thing, but it was one more disturbing sign that he was in trouble. It was a reminder that every time Jemima had to choose between him and her religion – he *lost*.

He pulled his mouth to one side. Out of all the women in the world, he had to fall in love with the most religious one. It was maddening. He'd met nuns who were more liberal than Jemima.

His expression softened. But Jemima was also the most beautiful girl on the planet, and the sweetest. And – she really loved him. Even if she hadn't told him so, he would've known. He could tell.

He could *feel* it.

He took a sip of coffee. He was ready to make his next move, but he had to go carefully. He was at a disadvantage in many ways: he was from the wrong culture, he held the wrong beliefs, he had the wrong career, and probably had the wrong *personality* thrown into the pot, too – just for good measure.

He shouldn't have had a snowball's chance with a girl like Jemima. But somehow, miraculously, he did. And he didn't intend to waste that chance.

He patted his lips with his napkin, motioned for the waitress and paid his bill.

He was going to go back to Lancaster County, red roses in hand, and pitch Jemima like he'd never pitched anyone in his life. Harder than he'd pitched the college admissions board, harder than he'd pitched Delores…harder than he'd even pitched *Jemima* before.

He was going to make love to her eyes, to her mind, to her heart. He was going to make the best pitch he'd ever made in his life – the best case a man ever made to a woman.

Because he was going in with two strikes against him –

and he knew it.

He put his card back into his wallet, turned up the collar on his coat, and shouldered out through the restaurant's big double doors. He walked to the corner and waited, shivering, until the light changed.

He paused for a moment in front of the jewelers', looked at the delicate ring sparkling in the window – and then walked inside.

CHAPTER TWENTY-THREE

Brad parked the truck in his usual spot, put on the parking brake and killed the motor. It was a few minutes before midnight, and Jemima was expecting him. He reached for a glossy cardboard bag on the driver's seat, reached in, and pocketed a small velvet box.

Then he grabbed a bouquet of red roses, and another box of the painted chocolates that Jemima had loved, and stepped outside.

The cold pinched his cheeks, his nose and his fingers. He sputtered, and could see his own breath in the frosty air. Lucky for him, there was a bright moon.

He chose to take the road this time, figuring that no one would be out in the snow at that hour. He also had no desire to wade through the brown brambles when he wanted to look his very best.

He walked briskly, and within minutes he was on the moonlit porch. He rapped cautiously on the front door, and it opened instantly. Jemima was standing there, smiling. She was framed by the muted light of a single lamp.

"Come in," she whispered.

They had decided to risk the house this time, partly because it was too cold for anything else, and partly because Brad had the strong sense that a marriage proposal should be made from the warmest, most favorable spot possible.

He held out the roses and smiled. "These are for you, Duchess."

"*Oh, Brad*!" She leaned over to kiss his cheek. "They're *beautiful*!"

She took his hand and led him to the couch, and they sat down. She leaned close and whispered in his ear: "We have to be *very* quiet. Deborah is watching upstairs, but if someone comes, we won't have much time."

"I'm not worried," he told her, and smiled again – as big and bright as he could.

"I was out shopping the other day, and happened across

these," he told her, and presented the box of chocolates. Jemima giggled and kissed him again.

He pulled off her cap, tangled his hands in her hair, and mussed it so badly that she pulled away from him, laughing, and pulled out the pins herself. That red gold tumbled over her shoulders and glowed in the lamp's warm light.

He played with a strand of her hair. "I can't stay away, Duchess," he told her. "You're the most beautiful woman I've ever met."

She colored, and dropped her gaze, but he took her chin in his hand and made her look at him. He held her eyes.

"*I love you, Jemima.*"

The smile faded from her lips and her eyes widened. She stared at him, searched his eyes.

"You don't have to check to see if it's true," he reassured her tenderly. "I mean it. Can't you tell? Doesn't *this* give you a hint?"

He took her by the shoulders and kissed her savagely, felt her gasp, and melt in his arms, and then open up to him like the rose that she was. She began to respond, to return his kisses, even to—

He checked himself, closed his eyes, pressed his cheek to hers.

"*Do you love me, Duchess?*" he breathed.

"*Oh, darling* – with all my heart!" she breathed. She twined her arms around his neck, as if to prove it, and pressed her lips to his ear.

It was a *good* sign. He took a deep breath, and decided to go for it.

"I came here tonight to ask you a question, Duchess," he smiled. "I hope you'll be kind to me."

He turned and kissed her again, and she murmured uselessly, and then put her hands in his hair.

When they parted again, they were both breathless. Brad smiled, and looked at her, and reached into his pocket. He opened his palm, and presented the little velvet box, and was gratified to see her beautiful eyes widen.

"Open it, Duchess," he told her. "This is for *you*."

She took the box reverently in her hands, and opened the little lid. Then she gasped and put a hand to her mouth.

Her voice was almost inaudible. "*Oh, Brad!*"

He leaned forward and put his hand on hers. "Will you *marry* me, Duchess?"

Those magical green eyes glowed with unbelievable fire. They met his, pooled with sparkling emerald tears.

"Oh, *yes*," she breathed fervently. "Yes, Brad. *Yes!*"

He sputtered with relief, cracked into a wide smile, put his arms around her, held her tight and rested his head against hers. *He couldn't believe it. It was a miracle!*

They kissed again, softly, deliciously. It was going to be the first of a lifetime of kisses, a glorious...

"Hissht!"

Jemima pulled back from him suddenly and turned to look at the stairs. A sharp, sly face appeared for an instant, and then was gone. It was followed by the unmistakable thunder of heavy footsteps, and they were travelling fast.

Jemima turned to him. "It's my father," she gasped, "Go, *quick*! I don't know *what* he'll do if he finds—"

Brad stood abruptly, but couldn't bring himself to leave. He'd only *just* won Jemima's agreement to marry him, and he figured it was bad luck to begin their engagement by treating Jemima to the sight of his back, running away.

Even if running away made *perfect sense.*

Jemima leapt up and clutched his arm just as Jacob King burst onto the scene like a giant from some fairy tale. His red hair was sticking out at all angles, he was barefoot, and—

Brad goggled at him. He was wearing a nightshirt. Even their pajamas were from the 1800s!

Jacob's outraged eyes took in the scene – Jemima's flowing hair, all undone, her rumpled dress, the bouquet of roses, the chocolates – and then they turned to *him.*

Jacob's red eyebrows descended in a thunderous scowl. His face gathered darkness, and he drew himself up until he towered over them like a storm cloud.

"I *knew* something strange was going on!" he burst out. "So! This is what my daughter does when she thinks her parents are asleep! She *cavorts* with a strange Englischer – in my very *living room*!"

Jemima burst into sobs and cast herself on her father's chest. She raised her hands to his neck, beseeching him in anguished German, but Jacob put her aside without a glance.

He turned his awful gaze full-bore on Brad.

Brad squared his shoulders, met the giant's eyes, and put out his hands in a calming gesture. "Mr. King, before you jump to *conclusions*—"

For answer, two massive hands grabbed him by his coat lapels and hoisted him up into the air. Brad suddenly found himself looking down into Jacob King's blazing blue eyes, and Jemima's horrified green ones, from just under the ceiling.

He dangled there for what seemed like eternity. Jemima was on her father's chest again, shrieking the word *verlobter* over and over again, to no effect, when a pretty blonde woman hurried into the room, dressed in a nightgown and a shawl.

She looked up at him with horrified eyes, rushed to the red

giant's side, and spoke to him in urgent German. For the first time, Jacob's menacing expression cracked. He turned his head and spoke a few terse words to her in German, and then raised his eyes.

Brad looked down into them and ventured diplomacy. "Mr. King, there's no reason for you to be angry. Jemima and I are *engaged*."

The word seemed to set his future father-in-law on fire. He jerked him higher, and his head bumped smartly against the ceiling.

"No daughter of *mine* is going to marry with a weaselly little Englischer reporter who makes his name off the misfortunes of others!" he thundered, "a fortune-hunting, fame-hungry, night-sneaking, fast-talking, dirt-eating, *schmutzig, wehleidig kleiner wurm!*"

With that, the red giant surged across the room, kicked open the door, took a running start across the porch and flung him into the blind night like a sack of potatoes. Brad sailed through the icy air, burst through a snowdrift, rolled over the edge of the lawn, fell onto the driveway, rolled a few more times, and came to a lumpy halt.

He raised his head painfully and looked back at the house through his hair. The door was still open, and he could see Jemima in it.

"*Brad!*" she shrieked, and made as if to run out after him, but someone pulled her back inside, and the door closed with a *bang*.

CHAPTER TWENTY-FOUR

The next morning Brad rose early, showered, shaved, bandaged his many scrapes and scuffs, and dressed smartly. Then he called in sick to work, and drove right back out to the King farm.

He pulled the truck up into the driveway, got out, walked stubbornly across the lawn to the front door, and rapped on it like a fearless man.

The sly-faced girl opened the door. She goggled at him for an instant, then drawled: "Well, you're brave – I'll say *that* for you."

"Where's Jemima?"

"Upstairs."

"Go tell her I'm here."

The girl shook her head and disappeared. Brad looked back over his shoulder, toward the workshop. The sound of vigorous hammering wafted through the open door.

There was a soft rushing sound inside, and Brad turned just in time to receive Jemima on his chest. She threw herself into his arms and covered his face with kisses.

"Oh my *darling!*" she cried, "Are you hurt?" She ran her small fingers over his face, and her mouth crumpled at the sight of a scrape across his jaw.

"Oh, Brad," she mourned, "I'm so *sorry!*"

Brad took Jemima by the shoulders. "Go get your things," he told her. "You're coming with me. I'm taking you back to my apartment until we get married."

But Jemima looked down at the floor and made no reply. Instead, the blonde woman that he assumed to be her mother appeared out of the kitchen, and invited him in.

"Why don't you come inside, Brad, and sit down?"

Brad shook his head. "I'm not here for a social visit," he told her, and turned back to Jemima. "Listen, Jemima, you're eighteen now, you don't need your parent's consent to be legally married. They can't hold you here against your will."

Jemima looked up at him pleadingly. "Come and sit down, Brad," she asked, *"please."*

The older woman beckoned, and after a long hesitation, he allowed himself to be led into the living room.

"I'm sorry for what happened last night, Brad," she told him. "My husband will be, too, when he's had time to cool down. Please, make yourself comfortable. I'll get something for you."

Brad sat down next to Jemima on the couch and turned to her, frowning, but she kissed the question right off his lips.

Mrs. King came back and set two cups of coffee down on the table before them, and a plate of peanut butter cookies. Brad glanced up at her with a look that communicated his sense of deep irony, but her manner remained placid and unruffled. She took a seat in a rocking chair across from the couch.

"You'll have to forgive us," she said quietly, "but last night was the first time that my husband and I even *knew* that you were courting with our daughter. It was quite a surprise to us. We assumed that Jemima would marry an Amish boy."

Her eyes moved to Jemima, and Jemima dropped her glance instantly. Then her eyes moved to Brad's.

"That's because, if Jemima marries a non-Amish boy, like you, it means that she will *not* be able to join the Amish church."

Brad turned to Jemima. She looked up at him pleadingly, and he read the truth of it in her eyes.

"It means that she will lose her place in this community, and her decision will be seen by others as a sign that she has turned her back on her faith. She will, in fact, be burning the only bridge that connects her to her faith, and to her God," Rachel explained.

Brad stirred and looked up at her. "I understand that's what *you and your husband* believe," he told her, with some heat, "but I don't share your views and I don't see why Jemima has to, either. If her family and friends think they should be able to pick who she *marries*, then maybe she's better off without them!"

Jemima turned toward him. "Brad, *please*," she murmured.

The older woman regarded him calmly. "Brad, when you ask Jemima to marry you, it isn't at all the same as asking an Englisch girl. You're asking Jemima to make a complete break with her past life. To abandon everything"—her voice cracked slightly, and she paused for an instant before going on—"and *everyone* she ever knew in her past. You might not have understood that, but we feel it *very* much. That's why her father was so – upset – last night."

Brad fell silent. He couldn't honestly say that he *had* understood that part. Jemima's eyes held unshed tears, and anger died out of his heart as he looked down at her. He hadn't really understood, until now, just *how much* he'd been asking her to give up. He felt his face going warm, and was struck with a sudden sense of his ignorance of Jemima's culture.

The sound of the front door opening made them all look up. Jacob King stepped inside and looked around for his family. When he caught sight of them all in the living room, he froze, wide-eyed.

Rachel was on her feet in an instant. "Jacob, *Jemima's fiancé* has come to pay us a call."

Jacob's voice seemed to rise up like a geyser, from deep underground. "*What is he doing here?*" he demanded, and began walking toward them.

A dark blur rushed past Brad's right shoulder. In an instant Jemima had moved between him and her huge father, and was staring up at him like a kitten challenging a bear.

"Daed, this is the man I've *chosen*," she quavered, "and I'm sorry if you don't *like* it, but Brad is my fiancé, and, and if you lay a hand on him *again*, I-I'll leave with him now and *never come back*!"

It was the only threat Jemima had uttered in her short life, but it froze Jacob in his tracks. He looked down at her, and then over at his wife.

"Come and sit down, Jacob," Rachel said softly, and touched his shoulder fleetingly with her hand. "I've been telling Brad about what it will mean to Jemima – and to us –

if Jemima marries with him."

Jemima returned to her place beside Brad on the couch, and reached for his hand. Jacob sat down in a big overstuffed chair, and regarded the two of them grimly.

"The only way I could *ever* approve of such a marriage," Jacob rumbled, "would be if the Englischer converted to the church. Then he and Jemima could *both* join, and be married. Only then."

Rachel nodded, and they both turned to look at him. To his horror, Brad felt Jemima's shy gaze on him as well. Surely *she* didn't expect him to convert, too?

Brad felt his mouth dropping open, and closed it. He sputtered incredulously, but the elder couple's grim expressions told him that no one in the room was joking.

Brad clawed at his collar, because suddenly it felt as if the room was closing in on him. He turned to Jemima.

"Jemima, this is crazy. I *love* you, and I'll marry you tomorrow if you get in the truck and come with me. But if you're expecting me to join your family's *religion*"—he threw out his hands—"I just – I can't *do* it. I don't believe in *any* God, and I could never live like *this*"—he gestured to the room around him—"like it was a *hundred years* ago!"

He reached for her hand and took it. "Let's get out of here," he urged softly. "Don't even worry about your stuff, I'll buy you new things. *Just come with me.* I love you,

Jemima. Come with me, *now*."

Jemima looked up at him with anguished doe eyes, and then looked at her parents.

"*Think* about what you would be doing, Jemima," her mother urged softly, "what you would be giving up *forever!*"

Jemima's eyes moved to her father's face. He looked at her with deep sadness. Tears shone in his weary blue eyes, and he rubbed them away with a big hand.

To Brad's dismay, Jemima put her hand over her mouth and burst into tears.

He leaned back into the sofa, stunned.

Once again, when it came to a choice between him and Jemima's religion – he'd *lost*.

CHAPTER TWENTY-FIVE

"Earth to Brad? Seriously – *wake up!*"

Brad snapped out of his daydream and looked up into Delores Watkins' disgusted face. She shook her head. "I don't know what's gotten into you, wonder boy, but it's reached the point that I don't care. If you don't start paying attention, I'm going to be the one sending *you* out to the sewage treatment plant!"

Brad shook his head. "Sorry, Delores. What was that again?"

She sputtered in exasperation. "I'll just send you an email. Assuming you still read *those*?" she snapped, and swept out of his office. The door slammed impressively behind her.

Brad closed his eyes. Delores was right, he was going to have to come back to his own life sooner or later. Sooner, if he wanted to keep his job.

He massaged his brow with one hand. He had an interview with the city mayor at 1 p.m., and he had to crank out a 1,000-word story after for the evening edition.

And he didn't know how he was going to do it. He was a *wreck.*

It had been a week since he'd driven the truck away from the King house, and he hadn't gone back. But yesterday he'd received a tearstained letter from Jemima.

He reached into his pocket, unfolded it on his desk, and read it again for the thousandth time.

Dear Brad,

I wanted to tell you I'm so sorry for all the bad things that have happened since you asked me to marry you. Please don't think hard thoughts about Daed, he is going to church tomorrow to repent and he is truly sorry.

Brad put a hand to his head and massaged the little throbbing spot between his eyes.

I didn't know what to say when you asked me to come with you. I love you with all my heart, and I want to marry you, but I love my parents too, and I love God, and I don't know what to do. It's true that you might not understand what it means for me to marry you, and how could you, you're not Amish, and I didn't want to harp on it or make you feel bad.

I wouldn't blame you if you never came back, or if you decided to break our engagement and find another girl. Like that blonde girl I saw you with once in town. She was very pretty and I could tell that she liked you a lot.

This part of the letter was heavily smudged, and was marred with watery blotches and signs of many revisions. Brad ran his thumb softly over the fuzzy lines.

I don't know what to do now, except to tell you that I will love you until I die. And to give you back the beautiful ring. I wouldn't be able to wear it anyway, because we don't wear jewelry, but I kept it under my pillow and looked at it a lot. But you might want to give it to some other girl, someday.

Brad sighed and reached into his pocket. He pulled out the little ring. Jemima had enclosed it in her letter. He turned it between his fingers, and it winked at him forlornly.

So if I don't see you again, I will understand, and I will pray that God sends you a beautiful Englisch girl who makes you very happy, and also that maybe someday you come to know Him, because that's what I have always prayed since I first knew you, and is the best thing that could happen.

So, if that is what you decide, I hope you go ahead with your own life, and forget you ever met me, and find someone who makes you happy. And I will go on, too, but I will always be glad that I found the George Washington letter, in spite of all the trouble it caused me, because it brought us together for awhile.

Love,

Jemima

Brad folded the letter carefully, put it back into his pocket, and pulled his hands over his face.

That evening, he stumbled through his front door and dropped his backpack on the floor. He'd been sitting all day, but he was bone tired. He stretched, massaged his back, and walked to the refrigerator. He pulled out a TV dinner, peeled back the plastic cover, and stuck it in the microwave.

The microwave beeped, and he pulled the tray out, stirred the contents, and brought it over to the table.

He looked down at his dinner. It was a disgusting brown blob.

Brad sank into a chair and poked at his food. He couldn't help wondering what Jemima was doing at that moment. Having dinner with her family? Or maybe, not *just* with her family. Maybe one of those Amish guys was there, too.

He picked up a plastic knife and fork and jabbed the meat patty. It wouldn't be long before they were all back at her house. Jemima's letter had made it clear that she was setting him free, and by implication, getting free herself. *That* news would travel fast.

He paused, staring vacantly into space. The thought of some other guy putting his hands on Jemima made him want to claw his own eyes.

But if he wasn't right for her, maybe he should be big enough to wish her happiness with someone else. Like she'd been trying to do for him.

He speared a chunk of meat and put it in his mouth.

After dinner, Brad went straight to bed and lay in his bed, staring at the ceiling. He was exhausted, but couldn't go to sleep for a long time. And when he finally did nod off, he was wracked by terrible nightmares.

He tossed and moaned on his pillow. He was back at the King farm again, and he was begging Jemima to come away with him, but it was like he was a ghost. No matter how he shouted and shook her, she gave no sign of having seen or heard him. She sat in her chair, sewing placidly, as if he wasn't there. Her parents sat beside her, reading, and no one paid any heed to him at *all*.

Then the door opened, and the dark-haired Amish guy came in smiling with a bouquet of roses. He presented them to Jemima. She took them shyly, and smiled back at him.

Brad ground his teeth, and *shook* her arm, and tried to get her to *hear* him, but instead, she stood up, and took the boy's hand, and they walked to the center of the room.

An elder appeared out of nowhere, an old Amish guy with a long white beard and a Bible. Jemima and the dark-haired guy stood before him, heads bowed, as he prayed over them. To Brad's horror, he pronounced them *married*, and Jemima's parents rushed over to kiss Jemima, and shake the boy's hand.

Then the smiling groom swung Jemima up in his arms, and carried her up the stairs and out of sight.

Brad sat bolt upright in bed, and yelled out hoarsely.

It took him a long time to realize that he was in his own apartment, and that it had just been a dream.

CHAPTER TWENTY-SIX

Brad went to work the next day and sleepwalked through his tasks. When he returned to his own apartment at the end of the day, he couldn't say that he'd accomplished much.

But even his own apartment had ceased to be a refuge. Brad tried to stave off the emptiness he felt by smoking; watching television, which he soon found unbearably irritating; and reading a book, which bored him.

He went to replace the book on its shelf and noticed his old photo album crammed in between a biography of Buckminster Fuller and a history of baseball. The album was skinny – he had very few photos of his own childhood, or of his parents. Most of the pictures had been given to him by his grandmother, or had been taken by her, and were relatively recent.

Brad opened the album, sat down on his bed, and sputtered out a wry laugh.

There was a wedding photo of his parents that his grandmother had kept. He stared at it, thinking that it must've been the only day in their married lives that they didn't fight. His Dad was wearing a brown tuxedo and a yellow boutonniere, and his Mom was wearing a white satin slip dress. She was holding a bouquet of yellow roses. They were both smiling, and his Dad's arm was around his Mom.

Then there was his own baby picture. He'd never liked that photo. He didn't know why his Mom thought it was cute to take a picture that he'd have to spend the rest of his life denying, but there he was, smiling up at the camera from a fake bearskin rug. His face hadn't been the only thing shining. He flipped the page.

There was the one school photo of him when he'd been in fourth grade, the one with his hair sticking almost straight up. He'd been wearing a goofy striped shirt that he'd had to pick out himself. To make things worse, the colors had faded strangely, and the photo looked almost pink now. He sputtered and shook his head.

That was the year Bobby Jenkins had tried to bully him, and he'd taught Bobby the definition of "left cross."

Brad moved the fingers of his left hand, and turned the page.

Then there was a picture of him and his grandmother. It had been taken by a friend of hers, not long after he'd gone to live with her. They'd been standing out in front of her little white house, on the lawn. He shook his head, thinking how skinny he looked, and his grams – he let his gaze linger on her face. She was scowling, her hair was pulled back into a severe bun, and her dress was a blue print bag.

He flipped the page, and smiled faintly. His grandfather's service medal was stuck in between the next pages. His grams had given it to him one day, long before he'd had any idea how big a deal that was for her.

"You never knew your grandfather," she had told him gruffly. "He grew up real poor. But he worked hard, and he *made* something of himself. See this? This is his service medal. He rose to the rank of a major in the Navy. It goes to show you what *you* can get, if you work hard."

She had pressed it into his palm, and leaned over and stared at him with an almost crazy intensity in her eyes.

"You take this. Maybe it'll remind you that you can make something of yourself, too."

He smiled faintly.

Yeah.

He flipped the page. There was his high school graduation photo of him standing there in his cap and gown. His grandmother had been by his side, but he'd had to hold her arm to keep her steady. By that time she'd been sick, and a month later, she'd been gone.

He still missed her.

He cut off that line of thought abruptly, flipped the book shut, and stretched out on the bed. He blew smoke contemplatively toward the ceiling.

The milestones of his life, in five photos.

But it was what had happened between the milestones, and the carefully posed portrait shots, that had shaped his life most. The things he didn't want to remember.

The things that had made an agnostic of him. He frowned.

Things like the recurring nightmare he'd had as a child, except that it had been *real*: the sound of his father screaming, of him knocking things off the kitchen table and yelling at his Mom. His earliest memories were of hiding behind the couch as his parents fought.

He took a pull at his cigarette. When he'd been very small, he'd prayed to God – he supposed because his Mom had taught him a bedtime prayer once and put the idea in his head. But if there *was* a God, He hadn't chosen to listen to those prayers. His parents' fights got more frequent and even more frightening.

One night when he was six years old, his old man had come home drunk and had beaten his Mom up. The sound of her screaming had driven him into the darkest corner of his bedroom closet, where he'd stayed all night with his hands clamped over his ears.

The next morning everything was deathly quiet. His Mom had been curled up in bed with a bruised face and cuts on her hands.

His Dad had gone, and he never returned.

Anger whisked up in him, like sparks from a lighter. He glared up at the blotchy ceiling of his apartment and prayed his first prayer in years. All the pent up resentment and rage of his childhood came pouring out suddenly, like flood waters breaking through a dam.

Why?

If You exist at all, why did You let all that happen? Why did you let my Dad take his issues out on Mom, and then leave us both alone? Why did You stand by when she started doing meth? Why didn't you save her?

Why didn't my Dad ever call me, even once? He didn't even come to Mom's funeral! If you're a God of love, why did You let all that mess happen?

Brad's mouth twisted down bitterly. *You abandoned us before Dad did.*

He lifted blazing eyes to the ceiling, and his face contracted in fury. *And how can you let an innocent girl like Jemima believe in the fairy tale, and sacrifice her own happiness because of it, when one day something will go so wrong that she'll see the truth? She'll see that there's nothing to all those stories she was told. But then it'll be too late to get back what she lost. It'll be too late to get back her life!*

What did she ever do to You?

If this is the kind of God you are, then You're a God of hate, not a God of love, and I want nothing to do with You!

Brad shook his head, and leaned over, and crushed out the cigarette.

CHAPTER TWENTY-SEVEN

"Darren! Darren -- don't!"

Brad moaned and tossed on his pillow. His mother's anguished screams filled his mind. He was a four-year-old again, hiding behind the couch as his parents fought.

There was a heavy, scraping sound, like heavy furniture being moved. Then another shrill scream, and a heavy crash, like someone falling to the floor.

More screams, worse than before, and the sound of heavy blows.

His dad's voice was thick, bleared, and rang out to the accompaniment of his mother's sobs. "I told you what I'd do if my dinner was cold again," he announced. "You've only got yourself to blame! I work my hands raw to put food on this table. The least you can do is make sure it's hot when I get home!"

"*Oh don't!*" his mother screamed, and his child-self clapped his hands over his ears again.

Brad moaned and tossed on his bed, and dug his face into the pillow.

His parent's living room melted, changed. The shouting faded to silence. The dull yellow lamplight gradually lightened to a wintry sky.

He was standing on the little stoop outside their back door. It was bitterly cold, but his mom was sitting on the steps, her shoulders slumped against the railing. And at seven years old, he knew what was wrong – when his Mom was crashing, she got so sleepy she practically passed out.

It was hard to move her, but he'd had practice; he opened the door, grabbed her feet, and slowly dragged her back inside again.

He had to stop and catch his breath. His Mom lay there on the kitchen floor with her arms splayed out, unconscious. Her face was gray, her lips were shriveled and dry, and her teeth were brown.

She looked older than his grandmother.

He'd crouched down and put his hand to her cheek, grieving for her. For the mother he should've had, and didn't. A hard lump burned in his throat.

He moaned in his sleep, hunched his shoulders over and settled onto his side.

The nightmare convulsed again, and now he was standing on a windswept hillside with his grandmother. It was cold and overcast, and he couldn't feel his fingers.

His grandmother had looked down at him, and for once, the look in her eyes had been soft. "You can *cry*, boy," she whispered, and squeezed his hand. But he'd cried himself dry long before he'd ever met his grandmother.

A minister stood in front of a big hole, and was praying over his mother's casket. And he had bowed his head, but he wasn't praying. He looked down into the hole and decided that there was no God, in spite of what his grandmother told him. No one could look down on that raw, gaping hole in the ground and believe in such a thing.

But he frowned, and thrashed, and prayed in his *sleep*.

Why.

Why.

Why.

Brad tossed, turned over on his back, and settled down with a sigh.

The dream vanished – and then began playing all over again. Brad gasped in his sleep, and thrashed.

No, no. No more.

He was back in his parent's living room. *"Darren! Darren – don't!"*

His mother's screams began again, and once again, he was a terrified four-year-old hiding behind the couch.

But this time, the dream was different. This time, he sensed the presence of a new participant. He raised his brows, and his eyes rolled underneath their lids.

There was light in the room now, not the dull yellow light of the lamp, but brilliant light – blue-white, dazzling. It blotted out the sight of his parents fighting, blotted out the sounds of his father's shouts and his mother's screams. It drowned everything else into oblivion – even his fear.

He saw his four-year-old self hiding behind the couch. And he saw a man standing beside him. The man reached down and put his hand on his head. He saw his child-self look up and smile.

He felt the old pain pouring out of his heart like black smoke, to be instantly swallowed up by the light.

Joy flooded his heart, and he didn't know why.

The light filled his whole mind, and the dream changed again. Gradually it resolved to the little stoop outside their back door. Once again, it was cold, and his Mom was slumped against the railing, in the throes of withdrawal.

And the light surged in like the sea. It streamed through the bare oak branches, consumed the ugly black railing, the concrete steps, his mother, and even him. And the man was there again, and looked down at him.

Unreasoning joy swelled in his heart, strained it, threatened to burst it – and the man laughed.

The old pain and the heavy grief burst out of his chest and flew away over the housetop like a flock of wild birds. And the joy threatened to overcome him.

An answering joy radiated from the man's face, and Brad looked at him in wonder.

The light blotted everything out and made his mind go white and blank. Then shape and color slowly returned. Once again, he and his grandmother were on the gray, windswept hill, and the minister prayed, and his child self looked down into the gaping hole in the ground. But now the man came and stood at his side, and wiped the face of the hillside with his hands. Light blurred the minister, blotted out the casket, filled the hole with light as if with water.

And then another white shape came and stood beside the man. Brad looked at the face that slowly resolved through the whiteness, the familiar eyes, and the smiling mouth – not shriveled now, not blighted, but young and radiant with life.

He fell to the ground and hugged his knees and moaned, crying like he'd never cried before – deep, wracking sobs. And the bitter anger spiraled up through his chest, was expelled with those sobs, and consumed by the light.

Brad woke sobbing. He sat up and reached wildly into the air with both his hands. The joy still glowed in his heart like a star.

But his apartment was dark and still. *It had been a dream.*

Brad sat in the dark, wide-eyed and panting. No, *not* just a dream. Because the old hurt, the old pain and fear were gone, as if the sea had poured through him and washed them away.

Even his *doubt* was gone.

He got up and turned on the light. He scrabbled over his bedside table for the one souvenir he'd brought from the green hill country: the plain brown book from his hotel room table.

He took it, and it fell open to a spot near the back. He looked down, and read:

"For God so loved the world, that he gave his only begotten Son, that whosoever believeth in him should not perish, but have everlasting life. For God sent not his Son into the world to condemn the world; but that the world through him might be saved."

Brad stared at the page through tear-filled eyes. The words pierced him, in their terrible beauty; his heart had been broken by joy, and emptied of grief, and now it was tender enough to be filled.

He bowed his head, and shook it in wonder. "You *are* real," he prayed in amazement. "I can't explain how, but I *feel* Your presence, and I know You're real."

He shook his head. "The pain is gone. It's *gone*. I don't know how – what did You do? – but I guess that part doesn't matter. The point is, I asked if you were real, and You showed me. I *believe* now."

Tears filled his eyes. "I may weaken later, but take my heart *now*, if you want it. It's not much, but I'll give it to You."

The joy came again, an echo of the joy in his dream, and he had the sense, somehow, that God was smiling. Brad closed his eyes and warmed himself in that glow. Then a new thought prodded him, and he smiled wryly.

Brad Williams – the *Christian*.

Who would've thought.

CHAPTER TWENTY-EIGHT

Brad pulled his truck to a stop in front of the King house. It was early twilight, a few days before Christmas. Snow covered the whole landscape, and the house looked like something from a holiday card. In the early dusk, the old homestead was a pale lavender, and warm golden light beamed from the windows.

There was a buggy parked in the front yard. Brad stared at it, frowning, and climbed out of the truck.

He knocked softly at the door and waited. He could hear the sound of many voices, and the scent of cinnamon escaped from inside.

The door opened, and Rachel King stood in the opening. Her eyes widened at the sight of him and her expression was one of surprise.

"I hope I haven't come at a bad time," Brad told her quickly, "but I'd *really* like to talk to Jemima."

Rachel hesitated for an instant, and then nodded. "Please come in."

Rachel opened the door and led him to where the chatter and laughter were coming from – a small room off the living room. Brad stepped in and drew a sharp breath.

The scene before him was straight out of his nightmare. Jemima was sitting in a big red chair, and there beside her was the dark-haired guy from his dream. Jealousy stabbed him. His rival sure hadn't wasted any time!

They both looked up as he entered. Jemima gasped and cried "Brad!" The smile faded off the other guy's face.

"Jemima, you have a visitor," her mother said quietly, and left.

The dark-haired guy stood up and turned to Jemima. "I'll go and see if Deborah has that book you were talking about," he said, and slowly walked out of the room.

They eyed one another uncomfortably as he walked past, and then he was gone.

Brad turned back to Jemima. Those huge eyes were on his

face and glowing like emeralds in the firelight.

"Come and sit down," she murmured.

He walked over and sat down in the chair beside her. The situation felt strained and awkward, but he plunged in.

"Jemima, I came here because I wanted to talk to you. I hope I haven't"—he tried not to grind his teeth—"*interrupted* anything?"

Jemima shook her head, and said nothing more. Her eyes were on his, as if she were trying to read them.

"I, um – I got your letter," he mumbled. "And I understand what you were trying to do. It was, it was very unselfish of you, Duchess. It was a beautiful gesture."

Jemima bowed her head, and looked down into her lap.

"But I came here to tell you that I don't *want* to be free. I want us to be married. More than anything in the *world*."

He reached over and took her fingers in his. They were trembling, and still she didn't meet his eyes.

"That is, if you still want to marry *me*."

She looked down at his hand. "But how, Brad?" she asked, in a small voice. "You don't want to live like me, and I can't live like you. How can we be married, if we can't live together?"

He ran his thumb gently over her fingers.

"Um…something happened this week, Jemima. Something happened to me that – well, I still don't how to describe it, but it – it made me see things differently. It made me think that maybe I can see things more like you. It made me – it made me—"

It was harder to say than he'd imagined. He closed his eyes and made himself do it.

"It made me believe that there *is* a God, after all. It helped me to trust Him. I, um, I-I met *Jesus*. As odd as that sounds."

Jemima's mouth had dropped open slightly, and she shook her head. "It doesn't sound odd *at all*," she cried, and tears spangled her eyes. "Oh, Brad, I've been praying for that for *months*!"

She threw her arms around him, and buried her head in his shoulder. To his amazement, she was crying. He put his arms around her.

"I just wanted to tell you that maybe we aren't that far apart anymore, in what we believe. At least *that*.

"And I've thought a lot about the other stuff. About my life, and my home, and my job. And, um"—he looked up at the ceiling in embarrassment, because there were tears in his eyes—"*none* of those things are as important to me as you are, Jemima. If I have to give them up for us to be married, I *will*.

"I'm not making any *promises*," he added quickly, in

response to her glad cry, "I can't promise that I'll be able to do it, Jemima. Just that I'm willing to *try*. I'm willing to start. If you'll help me."

"Oh, Brad," Jemima sobbed into his shirt, "*Help* you? Anything, anything, *anything*!"

Then she turned and gave him such a kiss, that he suddenly felt that he'd be able to live in a house on the *moon* – much less in a house off the grid.

Jemima laughed and took his hand. "Now come and talk to my family, and meet Mark. The two of you are going to be great friends."

He allowed her to lead him along, and they walked into the kitchen together, where their news was received by the family with joy, and a good bit of surprise. The sly-looking kid raised her eyebrows, as if she was out a bet; the mother burst out crying, and hugged Jemima; and the old man gave him a narrow look, grunted, stood – and stuck out his hand.

He had taken it, and tried not to wince when his hand was almost crushed.

He even took the dark-haired guy's hand, when he stuck it out.

"I'm Mark Christener," the guy had said.

He tried to think of something polite to say. "Nice right," he replied, and rubbed his jaw.

CHAPTER TWENTY-NINE

A year later, Jemima stood in her parent's living room, in her brand-new blue wedding dress. Bishop Lapp smiled down at her, and his bright blue eyes were full of the same joy that filled her heart. She looked over at Brad, so handsome in his black suit and bow tie, and with his shock of sandy hair.

It was their wedding day. Under usual circumstances, it never should have happened.

But *nothing* about their story had been usual.

As the bishop intoned the words of the blessing, Jemima thought back over the last year: all the things that had happened to make this day come true. Her Daed had built

Brad a little apartment addition onto the workshop, and let him live there while he was learning. He'd taught Brad how to help him in the shop, and so many other things: how to dress, what to do in worship, and what was expected of him as an Amish man.

It hadn't always been easy. They had fought *often*. Her father had threatened to throw Brad into the pond for his smart mouth, and his disrespect for tradition, and his rebellious attitude. And three times Brad had thrown down his hammer, and said he was going back to the Englisch.

But neither one of them had carried out their threats.

Maybe, she considered, the fighting had been necessary to make them respect each other. And then, to *like* one another. Jemima looked over at her father. He was sitting just behind them, wiping his eyes with a big brown hand.

Her mother had quickly come to love Brad. When she'd told her mother about Brad's childhood – or *lack* of one – Rachel had taken him to her heart immediately. And she knew he was fond of her, too.

As for Deborah – she still hadn't paid back the fifty dollars she'd wangled from Brad. But he didn't seem to hold it against her. In fact, Brad seemed to understand Deborah better than anyone else did, and even to *like* her. Which she had to admit, was kind of a rare quality.

She looked over at Brad, and caught his glance and smiled.

He gave her a look that promised great things later, and she lowered her eyes primly.

Brad had promised her nothing when he'd first come to live with them. But he'd stuck to his intentions more stubbornly even than she'd hoped. She'd probably never know how hard it had been for him to change to their ways. When he first came to live with them, Joseph had challenged him to a fight, and Samuel had accidentally knocked him into a pig pen.

But *none* of it had made him change his mind.

Gratitude welled up in Jemima's heart, followed quickly by joy. She closed her eyes.

Thank you Lord, she prayed. *Thank you for giving me the George Washington letter, because without it, I would never have met Brad. I couldn't see what You were doing at the time. I thought it was about the money, and I was unhappy for all the trouble it'd brought. But You never gave me the letter to make me a millionaire.*

You gave me the letter to make me rich in another way. To make us all rich.

She looked over at Brad again. He met her eyes, smiled mischievously and winked.

EPILOGUE

Former Reporter Marries Amish Millionaire

Serenity, PA – In a private ceremony conducted at the bride's home, Jemima King, best known as the Amish Millionaire, and Brad Williams, formerly of the *Ledger Enquirer*, were married this Tuesday. King first came to the attention of the public when the *Enquirer* broke the story of her rare find – a previously unknown letter from George Washington to his wife. King subsequently sold the letter at Brinkley's Auction House for $1.6 million.

Williams, at the time a *Ledger* reporter, met King in the course of reporting her story, and he also testified on her behalf when she was unsuccessfully sued for the money.

Williams resigned his post as an up-and-coming reporter for the *Ledger*, and has renounced modern life to convert to the Amish faith. He is one of the few people who have successfully made the transition to that way of life.

His former colleagues at the *Ledger* wish him, and his lovely bride, every happiness.

THANK YOU FOR READING!

And thank you for supporting me as an independent author! I hope you enjoyed reading this book as much as I loved writing it!

In the next chapter, there is a FREE sample of my new Christmas book, A Lancaster County Christmas Yule Goat Calamity.

If you like the sample, you can look for the rest of the book at your favorite online booksellers.

All the Best

Ruth

A LANCASTER COUNTY CHRISTMAS YULE GOAT CALAMITY

RETURN TO THE WORLD OF LANCASTER COUNTY SECOND CHANCES WITH ANNIE MILLER, A FIFTEEN-YEAR-OLD WILD CHILD WITH A GOAT-LOAD OF PROBLEMS!

Meet Annie Miller, a fifteen-year-old wild child with a Goat-Load of problems! After losing her mamm when she was only six-years-old, 15-year-old Annie Fisher and her family have managed to find some peace and happiness – even as Annie is viewed as a wild child by the rest of the community. But when Annie starts helping her daed out in his shop, things go from bad to worse when Annie accidentally wins an auction for five Nubian goats. Unable to return them or gain a refund, will this wild child find a way to sell the goats and rescue Christmas for herself and her family?

Find out in A Lancaster County Christmas Yule Goat Calamity by Ruth Price. This book is set in the same world as Lancaster County Second Chances.

CHAPTER ONE

The little bell over the shop door tinkled loudly, a current of cold air poured in, and Annie Miller stopped playing with a little ball and cup toy to see who was coming into her father's store.

Annie's bright blue eyes peeped out from behind the handmade brooms, but their expectant look quickly dimmed. It was only her cousin, Emma Lapp. Emma was nice enough, but she was *courtship* age. And that meant only one thing.

Poor Emma had *lost her mind.*

Annie gave her cousin a pitying look. All Emma ever talked about, all she cared about lately, was *boys*. She was dull as dirt – that was for sure!

Annie shrugged and went back to seeing how many times she could flip the ball into the cup. She was pushing a new record – 200 – and if she got it, she'd be sure to lord it over

Samuel Stauffer, because his record was 180, and he never let anyone forget it.

"Good afternoon, Emma."

Annie glanced up momentarily. Her father's redheaded employee, Daniel Gingerich, was standing at attention behind the counter and gazing down at Emma with that goofy look he always got when she came in. Annie frowned. She liked Daniel, but he'd turned into a real *goober* lately, and Emma was to blame. Not only was she boring, herself – she was spreading the infection to others.

"Good morning, Daniel."

"More of your friendship bread, I see! Your loaves just *fly* off the shelves during the holidays."

There was a soft simpering sound, and Annie rolled her eyes, and then spat out an exclamation, because she'd taken her eye off the ball and missed her shot – just shy of the record, too!

"I made an extra loaf for you, Daniel."

"Thank you, Emma."

A crinkling sound advertised the transfer of the gift from Emma's hands to Daniel's. Annie peeped at the counter from her hiding place and was astonished to see that Daniel's hand lingered on Emma's...*on purpose*.

She shook her head. It was a rotten shame: Daniel was a

sport and pretty good fun when he wasn't mooning over Emma, but bad was quickly turning into worse. The next thing you knew, he'd probably get all serious and start traipsing off to Emma's house, and stop joining snowball fights after work with the rest of them.

Annie calculated that it would probably be smart for her to start looking for next year's softball catcher too, before Daniel bailed, because she could see it coming. She made a mental note to choose a younger player next time, too, so she could count on at least a *few* steady years before the madness took hold.

"Are you coming to the sing this Sunday, Emma?" Daniel asked softly.

"Oh yes."

'Then I'll be there, too."

Emma giggled. "Oh, Daniel."

Annie, feeling she could stand no more, stepped out into the center aisle nonchalantly, but conspicuously. Daniel looked up and colored.

"Oh, there you are, Annie! I was wondering where you'd gotten off to," he said hastily.

She gave him a quick look, thinking that he should be ashamed to tell such a honking whopper, but only shrugged.

Emma turned and smiled at her. "Annie, Mamm has been

asking about you. She said that if I saw you, I was to ask you to come over for dinner this weekend."

Annie goggled at her pretty cousin in dismay. She had to think of an excuse, quick, or else her daed would make her go to her Aunt Katie's. But every time she went over there, they tortured her with soap and shampoo and brushing and braiding and all manner of foofy nonsense that made her wish that she could just run away into the woods.

"I-I'm sorry, I can't," she stammered, "I feel a cold coming on!"

She put a hand to her mouth and coughed. And then, because there were no excuses that worked better than her own feet, she turned and fled.

Daniel turned to Emma apologetically. "I'm sorry, Emma. She behaves more like a little squirrel than a little girl."

Emma stared at the shop door and shook her head. "Mamm is worried about her," she replied thoughtfully. "When Aunt Elizabeth died, there was no one left to teach Annie the things a girl should learn. And now she's 15, almost courtship age, and – look at her. Her hair coming loose, her dress all stained with grass and dirt from climbing and running. She doesn't even wear shoes until it gets cold."

She turned her lovely brown eyes back to Daniel. "What boy would ever want to court with Annie?" she wondered aloud. "She doesn't know the first thing about being a woman!"

Daniel shrugged and smiled. "Oh, she'll come around, Emma," he assured her. "When Annie decides she *wants* to court, she'll do what it takes to learn."

Emma shook her head. "Then she'll have to learn fast," was her worried assessment...

THANK YOU FOR READING!

If you enjoyed this sample, feel free look for the rest of the book in eBook and Paperback format at your favorite online booksellers.

All the Best,

Ruth

ABOUT THE AUTHOR

Ruth Price is a Pennsylvania native and devoted mother of four. After her youngest set off for college, she decided it was time to pursue her childhood dream to become a fiction writer. Drawing inspiration from her faith, her husband and love of her life Harold, and deep interest in Amish culture that stemmed from a childhood summer spent with her family on a Lancaster farm, Ruth began to pen the stories that had always jabbered away in her mind. Ruth believes that art at its best channels a higher good, and while she doesn't always reach that ideal, she hopes that her readers are entertained and inspired by her stories.

Printed by Amazon Italia Logistica S.r.l.
Torrazza Piemonte (TO), Italy